MOTIVE FOR MURDER

Salinsky flipped through his notebook. "You may be interested to know that others have expressed doubts about Mr. Humphries, specifically, Mrs. Morales, Dr. Morrow, Tallulah Spencer, Jake Spencer and Paolo Paolini."

"In other words, everyone in the house."

He nodded. "Everyone presently at home. Mr. Humphries is not well-liked, though being a fraud and being a murderer are two quite separate things."

"Hugh was so sick," I said. "How do you know he was murdered?"

"There are several indications that lead the medical examiner to that conclusion. There was an impression of your cousin's teeth on his upper lip, as if someone had pressed down hard on his face. There were goose feather particles and other textile matter in his airway. Hugh Morales was smothered with his own pillow."

"But why? He was going to die, and soon."

Salinsky closed his notebook. "That's the question, isn't it? Who benefits by your cousin dying days before he otherwise would have?"

Books by Barbara Ross

CLAMMED UP

BOILED OVER

MUSSELED OUT

FOGGED INN

ICED UNDER

Published by Kensington Publishing Corporation

Iced Under

Barbara Ross

KENSINGTON BOOKS

http://www.kensingtonbooks.com

KENSINGTON BOOKS are published by

Kensington Publishing Corp.
119 West 40th Street
New York, NY 10018

All Kensington titles, imprints and distributed lines are available at special quantity discounts for bulk purchases for sales promotion, premiums, fund-raising, educational or institutional use. Special book excerpts or customized printings can also be created to fit specific needs. For details, write or phone the office of the Kensington Special Sales Manager: Kensington Publishing Corp., 119 West 40th Street, New York, NY, 10018. Attn. Special Sales Department. Phone: 1-800-221-2647.

Kensington and the K logo Reg. U.S. Pat. & TM Off.

ISBN-13: 978-1-4967-0039-1
ISBN-10: 1-4967-0039-2
First Kensington Mass Market Edition: January 2017

eISBN-13: 978-1-4967-0040-7
eISBN-10: 1-4967-0040-6
First Kensington Electronic Edition: January 2017

10 9 8 7 6 5 4 3 2 1

Printed in the United States of America

This book is dedicated to Viola Jane Carito,
the funniest, smartest, most curious,
most wonderful granddaughter in the world.
Beautiful inside and out.

Chapter 1

Everyone who could leave town had left. The summer people were long gone, from the day-trippers to the seasonal home owners. Those retirees who could get out had gotten. My landlord, Gus, had run the restaurant downstairs from my studio apartment, offering breakfast and lunch, seven days a week for over fifty years. But in the last decade, he and his wife, Mrs. Gus, had closed down for the month of February and taken off to warmer places, visiting their adult children first in Arizona, then California.

My boyfriend, Chris, was gone too, helping some buddies move a sailboat from Saint John to Key West, so the winter restaurant Chris and I ran together, serving dinners in Gus's space, was closed as well. Chris had invited me along. It would've been our first trip together, but I could tell it was a guys' thing and declined. When I told him, his voice indicated disappointment, but as I'd expected, his green eyes glowed with relief. Let him and the guys have their fun. I was sorry not to get away, but not sorry to miss that particular trip.

Snow pelted the huge, multipaned front window of my apartment. It had been snowing forever, or at least it felt that way. We were in a weather pattern of heavy storms broken by a few days of sun and minor melting. Then, just as our spirits began to rise, the clouds arrived and the snow began again. The blanket of snow from the many storms, at least eighteen inches and counting, muffled sound and made the quiet little town of Busman's Harbor, Maine, even quieter.

My cell phone rang. My mom.

"Hullo, Julia. I'm home and feeling a little cabin-feverish. Would you like to come over for lunch?" Mom normally worked at Linens and Pantries, the big box store over in Topsham, but the winter storms had slowed commerce to a crawl. The busiest days required a staff of only two, so Mom had more time off than usual.

Lunch with Mom—why not? It was a five-minute walk over the harbor hill to the Victorian sea captain's home where I'd grown up. "Sure. What do you have to eat?"

I heard her rifling through pantry shelves. "Soup. Tuna." The *thunk* of the refrigerator door opening followed. "Eggs. Milk. Some lovely cheddar. There's plenty." She paused. "But you could do me one favor. Could you stop at the post office? It's been a couple of days and I'd love to get my mail."

"Mom, there's never anything interesting in the mail. It's all junk and catalogs." The trip to the post office would add a triangular, half-mile-long detour to my mother's house. I didn't relish trudging all that way in this weather.

"Please?"

What could I say? She was offering a hot lunch and companionship on a cold winter's day. And she was, after all, my mother.

After we hung up, I sat on my beat-up, old couch and pulled on my L. L. Bean snow boots. Like many Mainers, I had Bean boots for every type of weather. Le Roi, my Maine coon cat, spotted the boots and vocalized his displeasure. Maine coons are doglike in their desire for human company. I dragged a knuckle across his jowl. "Sorry, old man. Duty calls."

The hike to the post office was as treacherous as I expected. Most of the sidewalks weren't yet shoveled, so I walked in the road. The snow coming down hid bits of ice inside each flake, which burned when they hit my cheeks.

The town common was an unbroken field of snow, windswept into rows of rippling ridges resembling the white caps on the harbor. No one had even attempted to clear the little skating pond. The sledding hill was completely deserted, eerily silent. It was February school vacation week in Maine, yet even that hadn't brought the children outside into the wet, yucky snow. Perhaps they were gone too—off to visit grandparents in Florida, if they were lucky, or anywhere south of here.

The town common wasn't the business center of Busman's Harbor. That was Main Street, one block closer to the water, where, during the short summer season, tourists shopped in the little stores and boarded the tour boats at the pier. Most of the buildings around the common were homes, along with two white, steepled churches—the Congregationalists and the Baptists—and the library and post office. When I reached the PO, a thin light shone through the glass front door. *Neither snow nor rain nor heat nor gloom of night . . .*

The single public room of the post office was unusually empty. Along with Gus's restaurant, it was the place in town for news and gossip, catching up with old friends and making new, in the tourist season and the off-season. I stuck the key in my box and pulled out my mail. Nothing but junk, as I'd predicted. I stuffed the envelopes and catalogs into the Snowden Family Clambake tote bag I'd used as a purse since I returned to Busman's Harbor the previous spring. I went to the counter and called, "Barbara Jean? You here? I've come to fetch Mom's mail."

There was no response and I wondered where she could be. Then the back door opened and Barbara Jean McGonagle came in off the loading dock, boots wet, curly, brown hair covered with snow. "Sorry, Julia. I was helping Brett unload the truck. He got here late today because of the weather." She didn't ask what I wanted, but went straight to the back of Mom's box and emptied it. "This won't include today's. I haven't sorted it. Wait! I saw a package." She scurried toward a rolling mail cart that had high, dirty cloth sides. "I bet you're lonely with Chris away," she called.

I was saved from responding when she bent at the waist and dove so far over the cart I was afraid she'd topple into it. She emerged triumphant with a small package, which she handed across the counter to me.

The box was four-by-four inches square and about two inches deep, wrapped in brown paper and hand addressed to my mother in bold black letters. I looked for a return address. Nothing. Clearly, it wasn't from an online retailer. Had my mother been expecting it? Was that why she'd sent me on this otherwise foolish trip to the post office?

"No, I wasn't expecting anything. How intriguing." Mom deposited the little package on the kitchen counter. "I'll open it after we eat."

"You aren't going to open it right away? I went all the way to the post office in the snow."

She ignored my bid for sympathy. "It's probably nothing. You said so yourself. The mail is all junk." It was likely she was right. For many years, Mom had run the gift shop at our business, the Snowden Family Clambake, and vendors often tried to entice her with samples of their trinkets.

She'd already heated canned tomato soup and made up the grilled cheese sandwiches. My petite, pretty mother was many things. A cook was not one of them. Still, the meal she'd thrown together was better than I would have managed left to my own devices in my empty apartment. She had a particular twist on the sandwiches, which weren't so much grilled as broiled and included onion chopped and mixed with the grated cheddar. I bit into the gooey, tangy, crunchy goodness, and was warmed from the inside out—comfort food on a snowy day.

"Heard from Chris?" Mom asked.

"No, but it's only been a few days and I imagine cell coverage is pretty spotty where he is."

Mom nodded and shifted the subject. "I'm worried about your sister."

"Mom, all the worry about Livvie available in the universe is already being used by her husband." My younger sister and her husband Sonny were expecting a second child in two weeks, almost exactly a decade after the birth of their first, my feisty niece Page. Sonny was prepared, some would say obsessed. He had a plow fixed to the front of his big pickup truck and, ever since the string of snowstorms had started, he'd been hustling Livvie and Page out of the house for "practice runs," to the hospital. While weather was a factor, there was otherwise no indication that Livvie would have a problem with the birth. Despite the age spread between her children, she was only twenty-eight years old, two years younger than me, and in excellent health. She'd had some morning sickness in the beginning, but since then she'd had a model pregnancy.

"Livvie is fine," I assured my mother. "Can we open the package now, please?"

She sighed. "Very well."

I took our soup bowls to the sink and retrieved the brown-paper-wrapped bundle. When I picked it up, I ran my finger over the rough spot on the wrapping paper where the return address should have been. "You really don't know who it's from? A secret admirer?" I teased. "There's no return address."

My mother blushed. There hadn't been a man in her life since my father's death nearly six years before. "No, dear. I have no idea who it's from, but certainly no one like that."

"Open it." I jiggled in my chair with impatience. Her calm in the face of this mystery was driving me crazy.

Mom picked at the tape holding down one of the flaps and opened it.

"For goodness' sake, tear it," I said.

"Patience, Julia." She slid a box from the wrapping paper.

The box was generic, shiny and white, with no logo. Mom opened the lid to find a layer of cotton. She slid off the cotton and gasped.

The contents of the box glittered on a second bed of cotton—a necklace, judging from its length. The centerpiece was a huge black gem that looked like polished coal. It was surrounded by sparkling diamonds, and diamonds continued up the strand, at least two dozen total, though whether they were real or fake, I couldn't tell.

Mom pulled the necklace from the box and held it up. The diamonds sparkled, and light glinted through the huge black gem at the center. So much for my secret admirer theory. No one who knew Mom could think she would wear something so large and show-offy—or that she would have any place or occasion to wear it.

"Do you think it's real?" I asked, my heart beating faster at the mere idea. It couldn't be, could it? Mom's mouth hung open. She hadn't said a word. "Mom?"

"Yes, it's real," she answered. "The necklace is called the Black Widow. It belonged to my family."

Chapter 2

"Oh, my gosh, have you seen it before?"

Mom shook her head. The color had drained from her normally pale face, and the slim hand that held the necklace shook slightly. "It's been missing for almost a hundred years."

I took the box and scrabbled through the cotton bedding, looking for a note. Underneath was a card, thick, off-white, and expensive. In black ink, in bold handwriting with squared-off letters, the note contained two words.

I passed it silently to my mother, who read aloud: "'For Windsholme.'"

Windsholme was the name of Mom's family's old mansion on the private island where we ran the Snowden Family Clambakes during the tourist season. While we'd continued to use the island, the enormous summer house had been closed up and empty for years. Last summer a big part of it had burned, including the grand central staircase. At the end of the season, we'd boarded it up to keep the winter elements out and put off deciding what to do about it for the future. I knew in my heart that despite my boyfriend, Chris's, optimism that it could be rebuilt, and despite my mother's heart's desire, the practical thing, the only thing, was to tear it down.

"Julia, you have to help me find the person who sent this." Mom's voice was even, but her bright blue eyes pleaded.

I took the necklace from her and held it in front of me. It was heavy. I imagined it would get tiring to wear. "Tell me what you know about it."

"Let's have some tea."

I couldn't tell if Mom craved tea or if she needed a moment to gather her thoughts, so I didn't badger her while we waited for the kettle to boil and she went through the ritual of pouring the cups. The tea made, Mom led the way to our infrequently used living room and settled on the couch. The gray skies outside the big windows let in little light, but she didn't turn on the lamps. I took the box, the wrapping paper, and the necklace and followed her, settling into the deep chair across from where she sat.

"I don't know much at all." Her statement didn't surprise me. Her mother, Ellen Fields, née Morrow, had died when Mom was five. Mom was raised by her quiet, distant philosophy professor father and a succession of housekeepers. Whatever family history his wife had passed on to my late grandfather, he hadn't passed any further.

"Tell me what you do know," I coaxed.

"This is the Black Widow, a necklace with a rare black diamond at its center, which belonged to my ancestors." My mother reached across the coffee table and took the necklace from me. "At least I think it is. It could be a copy, of course. The Black Widow may not have even looked like this. I've never seen a photo, only heard it described. It disappeared from Windsholme and Morrow Island sometime in the 1920s, I believe. A housemaid was suspected, because she had left the island the night it was last seen to visit her family on the mainland and didn't return to work the next day or ever again. But she was never charged and the Black Widow was never found. Honestly, that's all I know."

"Who told you this?"

"My cousin Hugh, though I believe there are many who know the story." She turned the necklace in her hand.

"Oh." The topic of my mother's cousin, Hugh, was not one I was anxious to explore. He, like the Black Widow, had disappeared off Morrow Island, though in his case it was in 1978, on the night of my mother's twenty-first birthday. Even after all these years, the mention of Hugh brought tears to Mom's eyes. I'd always assumed that he'd drunk too much at my mother's party and had fallen off the cliff face, though no body had ever been found. It was clear my mother felt somehow guilty about it, like having a twenty-first birthday party made her responsible.

I left the subject of poor cousin Hugh aside

for a moment. "We'll keep everything, the box, the cotton, the wrapping," I said, "and see what we can figure out."

"Do you think your police friends can help us?" Mom asked.

"I don't know." Since I'd returned to Busman's Harbor the previous March, for reasons far beyond my control, I'd helped a team of state police detectives with more than one murder investigation. "Usually you contact the police when something is taken, not when something unexpectedly shows up. Let me work on it."

I climbed the main stairway to the second floor and entered the room at the front of Mom's house. Though I'd moved to the apartment over Gus's restaurant in the fall, this was the place where I ran the clambake business. The office had been my father's before it was mine and it still held his old metal filing cabinets and enormous mahogany desk. I went to the big front window and looked through the falling snow down the hill to the town pier and the Snowden Family Clambake ticket kiosk, standing at the ready, waiting for spring.

I fired up the desktop computer. It was old—I had a newer, sleeker laptop back at my apartment—but more than sufficient for my purposes. When the monitor sprang to life, I typed "Black Widow necklace" into a search engine.

There were no results, or at least nothing the

least bit useful, just a lot of Halloween costume jewelry, as well as discussions about a necklace Scarlett Johansson's character had worn in the Marvel *Avengers* movies.

So I typed "black diamond" to see what I could learn. Black diamonds did occur in nature and were exceedingly rare and beautiful. There were some famous ones, though I didn't spot the central stone of the Black Widow among the images. There were also man-made black diamonds, still expensive, but a fraction of the value. And there were fakes, big black stones in costume jewelry, apparently favored by witches and Goths.

The Internet had gotten me nowhere. I went downstairs and put the box with the necklace in it, along with the wrapping paper, in my tote bag. Mom was in the kitchen when I brought my boots from the back hall to put them on. She said, "Are you going out? I'd hoped you'd stay for the afternoon."

"You want to know where the necklace came from," I reminded her. "I'll be back."

"It's getting worse." Mom inclined her head toward the kitchen window. The sky was a dark gray and the wind had come up, pushing the icy snow sideways against the glass.

"I won't be long."

Chapter 3

I walked carefully down the hill that led from my mother's house to the commercial part of Main Street. On the corner of Main and Main, where the street snaked around, following the contour of the harbor hill and crossed itself at the only traffic light in town, was Gordon's Jewelry, my destination. I only had my mother's speculation that the Black Widow was genuine and had been in her family. She'd never seen the real thing, for one, and even she had said the necklace might be a copy.

I half expected the shop to be closed, given the awful weather. It was the off-season, and both Christmas and Valentine's Day had gone by. It was hard to think of a reason why Mr. Gordon would stay open, but when I pushed through the front door, there he was at his desk, jeweler's loupe to his eye, studying some items on a felt cloth in front of him.

He looked up, startled to see me there, despite

the opening and shutting of the shop door. "Julia Snowden. What brings you out on such a terrible afternoon?"

"I'm surprised to find you at work."

"Better than staring at the four walls at home." He expressed the Mainers' disdain for wintry weather. "What can I do for you?"

"I'd like you to look at something, if you have time."

"Nothing but time." He gestured around the empty store. He was a small, round man with twinkly blue eyes that were usually hidden by the thick glasses he put on when he removed the loupe. His white hair was longish, hanging over his ears. When he got up, he took the pieces he'd been studying, which turned out to be a pair of emerald earrings set in gold, and returned them to one of the shop's glass cases, locking it as he did. The tidy habits of a man who'd handled valuable things all his life.

He looked at me with interest across the counter. "What have you got for me?"

I slid the box out of my tote bag and onto the glass counter. I opened it, removing the top layer of cotton.

"Jeezum crow, Julia. What have ya there?"

"That's what I hoped you could tell me. Is it real?"

"May I?" He gestured toward the box. I nodded and he picked up the Black Widow with both hands, carefully balancing the big center gem as it dangled from the diamond-encrusted strands. He took the necklace to his worktable, put the jeweler's loupe back on, and examined it with a couple of instruments I didn't recognize. "It's real, all right. Where did you get this?"

"It came to my mother." I told the truth, but what I said was deliberately misleading. I hoped he'd think that it came to my mother through inheritance.

He didn't ask me more, but returned to studying the necklace intently. "Beautiful setting. Antique, as are the stones. You can tell by the way they're cut. Not this century or the last one. Late eighteen hundreds, I would say."

"What's it worth?"

"I couldn't begin to tell you. Pieces like this are hard to value. That center stone is rare, for a certainty. A true black diamond. Enormous. Seventy carats. And it's surrounded by"—he counted—"two dozen genuine white diamonds. I've been in the trade all my life, and I've not seen the like of it."

"Is it worth ten thousand dollars?" I put a stake in the ground.

Mr. Gordon gestured with his thumb, upward.

"One hundred thousand?"

Upward.

"Five hundred thousand?" I could barely get the words out.

More.

A swishing sound pounded in my ears. "A million?"

He nodded. "Closer. I would guess around two million."

I could barely catch my breath. "You're kidding." Someone had sent it through the mail, uninsured, with no return address.

He put his glasses back on. "You say this is your mother's? It must be listed in some estate inventories. And if it ever went to auction, it would appear in the catalog, depending on when it was bought."

"My mother said the necklace was called the Black Widow. Have you heard of it?"

Mr. Gordon shook his head. "Never. And that's odd, because I've appraised, or at least seen, most of what's valuable in these parts. How did you say you got it?" He peered at me, gray eyebrows drawn together over his glasses' frames. He was a nice man, a man whose discretion could be trusted with all sorts of information— from who in town owned something of real value, to who was about to pop the question. But it was widely known my mother's family hadn't had any real money since the 1920s. And since we'd almost lost my mother's house, Morrow Island, and our business to a loan default the previous spring, if we'd had a resource like this at the time, why wouldn't we have used it?

"It was in my mother's family," I answered, blushing deeply. I was lying, or at least not telling the whole truth, and I could tell he knew it.

He put the necklace back in the box, covered it, and slid the box back into my tote bag.

I couldn't look him in the eye. "Thank you."

"That necklace needs to be formally appraised, Julia. It should be insured and put in a safe deposit box. Don't you go walking around with that thing."

"I'll take care of it right away." I made for the door.

"Careful as you go, Julia," he called after me. "Careful as you go."

I walked into the street. The town plow churned by, heading up the hill toward Mom's. It felt weird, to put it mildly, to stand at an intersection in my little town with two million dollars' worth of diamonds in my Snowden Family Clambake tote bag. I felt nervously for the box to make sure it was still there, that I hadn't lost it in the four-foot journey from the jewelry store. I had one more errand to run before I took it home.

I headed back to the post office, walking in the newly plowed street. It was almost five o'clock and nearly dark. We'd gained daylight rapidly since December, but as far north as we were, as far east in our time zone, the days were still brutally short. I jogged along as best I could on the crunchy ice in the street, fingering the necklace box every few feet as I ran, reassuring myself it was still there.

It was hard—no, impossible—to wrap my head around the life-changing possibilities of two million dollars. When we'd rescued Morrow

Island, the clambake, and Mom's house from the bank in the spring, we'd done so with a loan from my friend Quentin Tupper. Quentin had lent the money unselfishly, because he was a friend, and because he had more money than he knew what to do with. And he knew, over the long term, we were good for it. But he had also done it selfishly, because his land looked right across at Morrow Island and he feared a high-end resort, complete with helicopter pad, would be developed there. I'd envisioned paying Quentin off slowly and painfully, over many years, with the profits from the clambake company.

At the end of last season, Mom, Livvie, Sonny, and I had taken the bare minimum of money we could and sent the rest to Quentin. That meant I was running a winter restaurant, Sonny was back doing dangerous work on his father's lobster boat, and Mom was toiling at Linens and Pantries. When I heard the magic words, "two million dollars," I imagined Quentin paid off and my family living comfortably off the clambake's profits, with plenty of money left over for Page's education, and the new baby's.

"Hullo?" I called when I entered the post office. The sounds of packages being moved came from the back. "Hullo?"

Barbara Jean emerged, curly hair wild, looking harried. "Julia, you're back. I didn't expect to see you again quite so soon." She glanced at the time. "I've already clocked out. I'm not allowed to stay late. The USPS insists I leave at five." She rolled her shoulders. "They're afraid I'll try to make them pay overtime."

"I hope this won't take more than a minute." I pulled the brown paper wrapping out of my tote. "I'd like to know where this package came from."

She squinted at me. "Sure, but why?"

"There was a gift in it for my mother, but the sender didn't include a card and there's no return address. She wants to send a thank-you note." *A big one.*

"Of course." Barbara Jean pulled the glasses from the top of her head. "Let me take a look." She stared intently at the wrapping paper. "For one thing"—she pointed to the corner of the front—"this is a precanceled stamp. That's why you don't have a postmark." When I looked puzzled, she said, "Precanceled stamps are the kind you buy in the automated machines." She nodded toward a kiosk standing by the PO boxes, then returned her attention to the wrapping paper. "Hmm. The originating zip code has been blacked out." She pointed to a thick black line on the stamp. It looked like someone had run a Sharpie over it. "And we're not supposed to accept packages with precanceled stamps unless they have a return address."

"So this shouldn't have been shipped this way?"

"No. But there aren't enough inspectors to catch everything." She ran her finger over the rough patch on the wrapping paper. "It looks like it did have a return address sticker, but it fell off. See the adhesive and the bit of paper backing here."

"Does all this mean you can't tell where it was sent from?"

"Not right this minute, but the sending post office would be encoded in these numbers on the precanceled stamp. I can find out." She looked up at the big clock on the wall. "But not today. I've already shut down my system. Bring it back on Monday. I'll dig into it then."

"Can you at least tell me *when* it was sent?"

"Come back Monday morning, first thing," she promised, gently pushing me out the door.

Chapter 4

I ran back to my apartment to make sure Le Roi had plenty of food and water, and then continued on to Mom's. It was fully dark by the time I reached her house. Normally, I would have gone in the back door, but the long walk down the unplowed driveway didn't appeal. Whatever I did, I'd have to climb over the huge mound of wet snow the town plow had pushed up against the curb, while clutching my tote bag and its precious contents in my gloved hands.

I took a deep breath, climbed the snow mound, sunk in snow up to my thigh, and then trudged up the steps, onto the front porch, and pushed open the always-unlocked front door.

"It's me!" I stomped my boots on the mat before entering.

"Upstairs," Mom answered.

I found her in the sitting room off her bedroom, a book in her lap and the Weather Channel playing silently on the TV. "The storm

will go all night," she said in hushed tones.
"You'll stay?"

"Sure. Let me find something dry to put on
and do a little more work. Then I'll come back
and tell you what I've discovered."

Her eyes widened, and I wondered if she'd
demand to know what I'd found right that
second, but I was obviously wet and cold, so she
let me go. I hurried into my old room, which
was still covered with rose print wallpaper and
furnished with a single twin bed. I pulled an old
pair of pajama bottoms out of a bureau drawer.
I'd stayed in this room from March until Octo-
ber and hadn't taken everything when I moved
out. I paired the pajama bottoms with a long-
sleeved Snowden Family Clambake T-shirt and a
ratty sweater that should have been heaved
years before. I longed for a hot shower, but I
had one more thing to do before I talked to
Mom, and the later it got, the lesser the odds I
could accomplish it.

I crossed the hallway to the clambake office,
tote bag in hand. My parents had started the
business in the 1980s, just before the explosion
in credit card use. In those years, during the
summer season, the clambake generated a lot of
cash. Also back then, banks were closed on Saturday afternoon and all day on Sunday, the two
busiest days at the clambake. So my father had a
safe in his office, a sturdy model that sat on the
floor beneath the desk. We didn't keep much
cash in the house anymore. There was much less
of it used at the clambake, for one thing, and a

deposit went to the bank every night. But the safe had stayed, probably because it was too heavy for anyone to move.

I turned on the desk lamp, then twirled the combination on the safe's lock—a string of family birthdays—and pulled open the door. There wasn't much inside. My mother's passport, and my dad's, which gave me a pang of sadness to see, their wills, the deed to the house, and some other old papers. I opened the white jewelry box, made sure once again the Black Widow was inside, replaced the lid, and put it in the safe. I twirled the dial around to obscure the last number of the combination, sat back in the desk chair, and pulled out my cell phone.

While the phone at the other end rang, I listened to the old wooden storm windows rattle in the wind. I could feel the gusts sneaking through the crevices.

"Cuthbertson here."

"It's Julia Snowden. What are you doing? Is this an okay time to talk?"

"Julia, I am doing what any sensible person would be doing at this very moment. My feet are up, the fire is lit, I am drinking coffee brandy and watching a basketball game I care nothing about whatsoever. It may even be a rerun."

"So it is okay to talk?"

"Fire away, my dear, though I hope you're not calling me from some county jail, because I'm too comfortable to come and get you. And I may have had a little too much of the aforementioned coffee brandy to drive in this weather."

Cuthie was a short, round man, with a head full of thick, mahogany brown hair that was always coated in a "product" that smelled like Vaseline. His clothes were miles too big and hung on him like pajamas. But appearances to the contrary, Cuthie was a brilliant criminal lawyer. He had helped me, my family, and my employees out of several jams.

"It's not actually a criminal matter," I said, "but you're the best person I can think of to call."

"I'm intrigued. Proceed." He had a deep, resonant voice he used like a weapon in the courtroom.

"Say someone sent you something valuable in the mail, anonymously. Is it yours to keep?"

"The US Mail or a private delivery service?" he clarified.

"US Mail."

He was silent for a moment. "How valuable?"

"Seven figures."

He whistled. "Is it cash? Because the federal government takes a dim view of that amount of cash going through the US Mail."

"No. Not cash."

"Stock certificates? Bearer bonds? Money orders? Because that stuff has particular rules."

"Nothing like that."

"Whew. This is fun. Is it a deed to a piece of property?"

"No."

"Okay, we're making progress. Is it a physical item, like a coffee can full of gold doubloons or a ruby-encrusted tiara?"

"Yes, more in that neighborhood."

"Interesting. And was this package addressed to you? Because if it was addressed to someone else and delivered to you by mistake, that's a different kettle of fish."

"It was addressed to my mom. I'm asking for her."

"And she has this ruby tiara in her possession right now?"

"Yes."

"Possession does make a difference in these cases. Certainly, you have a claim. The legal question is, do you have the best claim? How many people have as good or a better claim? With that kind of value, as soon as anyone knows you have the tiara, claimants will crawl out of the woodwork. These cases are almost always huge messes, and as a result, almost always get settled, with the item being sold and the money divided up." He paused. "Of course, if it was stolen by the person who mailed it to your mom, and there's one person who can prove he's the rightful owner, all bets are off. It's not yours at all."

It was my turn to be silent.

"Did I answer your question?" Cuthie asked.

"Yes."

"In that case, it was lovely talking to you. When you're finished wearing the tiara around the house, be sure to put it in a safe place."

"Already done," I answered.

* * *

Mom waited in her armchair in her sitting room, a shawl across her shoulders and a blanket spread out on her lap. In the light of the single lamp beside her, she was practically invisible in her deep, pink chair.

The room was an old sleeping porch my parents had "winterized" sometime in the late eighties. Outside, the branches of the tall pines that divided our yard from the neighbors *whooshed* and crackled.

I didn't take the empty chair beside her, but instead, sat on her ottoman so I could look her in the face. "Mom, Mr. Gordon says the necklace is real, every gem in it."

"I thought so from the first."

"It's quite valuable."

She shrugged. "Well, it would be."

I smiled a little. "How valuable do you think it is?"

Mom cast her eyes heavenward. She hated guessing games. "A hundred thousand dollars?"

"Two million."

That got her attention. She sat forward so quickly the blanket fell from her lap. "You're joking."

"I'm not. It wasn't a proper appraisal, of course, just his best guess. It could be quite a range, but we need to face the fact that someone, somewhere, put that necklace in a box, without insurance, or tracking, and sent it to you, using your proper name and your correct PO box number."

She blinked a few times and then the power surged, snapping off the silent TV, and momentarily brightening and then dimming the lights before they returned to normal. Without even looking, Mom opened the drawer in the end table by her chair, pulled out a flashlight, and set it on the tabletop. "My heavens. We have to figure out who sent it."

"I agree. I talked briefly to Cuthie Cuthbertson. He said you would have a claim to the necklace, since you possess it, but whether it's really yours would depend on whether someone had a better claim. So, I think we have to do that, Mom. Figure out who might have a better claim."

My mother chewed on her lower lip. I waited while she processed the information I had given her. It was a lot to take in. I'd had over an hour with it, and I was still processing.

"It's important to find out whom the necklace belongs to, I agree," she finally said. "But there's a more important reason to find the sender. Whoever it is, is most likely a member of our family."

"Why do you say that? What about the story that a housemaid stole it?"

"I don't think that explanation could be true. A poor woman's family never would have kept the Black Widow all these years as a souvenir. If a maid had taken it, it would've been fenced immediately, and it probably would have resurfaced sometime between then and now." Mom looked down at her hands in her lap. "I think the necklace must have been with someone in the family the whole time. That's the only way anyone would have sent it here to me." She looked back up at me. "Julia, you have to help me find my family."

I knew how much my mother longed for a connection to family, cut off when her mother died, found via her cousin, Hugh, and then lost again with his disappearance. Mom was right. I did have to help her find her family. She needed it, and there were practical considerations too. Two million dollars' worth.

I squirmed on the tufted pink ottoman. "You said your cousin, Hugh, first told you about the Black Widow. We're going to have to talk about him."

My mother nodded to show she understood.

"My first question is, how is Hugh even your cousin?"

As the words came out of my mouth, a mighty gust blew outside. The lights brightened, dimmed, brightened, and went out.

Chapter 5

When you live at the end of a peninsula, literally at the end of the road, power outages are a fact of life. My mother was prepared. A half hour later, we were seated in front of the living room fireplace, a roaring fire burning on the hearth. We'd made peanut butter sandwiches for ourselves and heated hot chocolate on Mom's gas stove, converted to run on propane since gas lines didn't come all the way into town.

Mom had called Livvie to check on her. She, Sonny, and Page were fine, but also without power, even though they were twenty minutes farther up the peninsula. Mom had also checked on our neighbors, the elderly Snugg sisters across the street. They were also fine, though their Scottish terrier was refusing to go out in the storm and his situation was increasingly desperate.

I hoped the relative darkness of the room, lit only by the glow of the fire, would make it easier

for Mom to talk about Hugh. My mother was
an only child, and her mother, Ellen Morrow
Fields, had been an only child as well. That was
why Mom owned Morrow Island, because her
mother had been the only heir. Hence my question, how was Hugh a cousin?

"Hugh and I met at boarding school," Mom
said. "We were in the same biology class our
freshman year. When the instructor called the
roster the first day, he read out full names.
When he said my name, 'Jacqueline Morrow
Fields,' a boy turned to stare at me. Later in the
alphabet, when the instructor called out 'Hugh
Windsholme Morrow,' it was my mouth that
dropped open. After class, Hugh approached
me and said, 'I think we're cousins.'"

I marveled at the coincidence of this. Mom
had gone to the same prep school I had, the
same one as her mother. It was the sister school
of the one attended by her grandfather, so there
was a family tradition that Hugh's branch might
also have been part of. But my mother had gone
there only a few years after the brother and
sister schools had merged. Five years earlier
and there would have been no shared biology
class, no shared campus, just a few annual
dances. She and Hugh might never have met.

Mom nestled back into the couch, relaxing
with the telling. "It took us a while to figure out
exactly how we were related. I, of course, had no
one to ask, my mother being gone and Dad
being absolutely hopeless with that stuff. Hugh
was for some reason reluctant to ask his parents

about it, but he knew a bit more than I did. His branch of the family was in San Francisco. His ancestors had gone out there in the nineteen-teens, chasing a fortune, which they, in fact, had made. They came east infrequently after that, but he'd heard of Windsholme. It was natural to be curious. It was his middle name. His ancestors had stayed there frequently, until sometime in the 1920s, when there was a terrific rift, and the two branches of the family never spoke again."

I counted on my fingertips. "So that made you and Hugh, what, third cousins?"

"Yes. Our great-great-grandfathers were brothers."

"So, not very close."

"No, but remember, at the time I thought I had no living relations on my mother's side. I barely remembered her and was eager for a connection. Besides, Hugh was such a sweetheart. A nice, nice guy. Smart, funny, good-looking. He made friends easily, and since I was more reserved, I was happy to be taken under his wing. At the end of the school year, I invited him to visit Morrow Island. I thought he should see Windsholme for himself since he was named for it. We took the train together. Your grandfather picked us up in Portland. Hugh helped us open the little house together, and then he stayed. He stayed the whole summer and all the summers after. He came to our apartment in New York for several Thanksgivings, Christmases, and spring breaks too."

My mother had teared up as she spoke and I

hesitated to push her. But she looked me full in the face, inviting the next question.

"It seems odd he would spend so much time with you and Grandfather. Hugh was at school all the way across the country from his parents. You'd think they'd want to see him on his vacations." I didn't add what I really thought, which was that it was hard to imagine someone wanting to spend their holidays with my distant, cold grandfather. And that, with Windsholme long closed down, the little house by the dock on Morrow Island where my mother and her father spent the summers didn't offer an extra bedroom for a distant cousin, only a daybed in the living room. I was sure Mom and Hugh had been close friends, but I couldn't understand why he'd have spent so much time with her family.

Mom hesitated. "I knew there were problems between Hugh and his parents. It wasn't something he liked to talk about, but I gathered they had problems of their own. His father was tyrannical and controlling, and his mother small-minded, very concerned about the opinions of others. That clashed with Hugh's personality, which was adventurous, open, up for anything, interested in everyone. I don't know the details, but I do know it was a most unhappy family."

"And then he disappeared," I prompted. On the one hand, this story was a legend in our family, but on the other, I had never heard any details, certainly not from my mother's lips.

Mom nodded and soldiered on. "It was on my twenty-first birthday. Your grandfather had given me a party on Morrow Island. It was not something he would normally do, or had ever done before, but I guess my twenty-first was important to him."

To me, Mom's father had always seemed disengaged and vaguely befuddled. He handed Livvie and me twenty-dollar bills on our birthdays, blinking through his thick glasses as if he was astonished to be related to us. Or to my mother, for that matter. But though I'd always felt sorry for Mom growing up with this strange man and a revolving series of housekeepers, she spoke of her father only with love, both when he was alive and in the eight years since his death. Throwing her a twenty-first birthday party was not completely uncharacteristic of him. I'd heard of evidence of this behavior before, for example in his insistence that my mother attend the dances at the Busman's Harbor Yacht Club. It was as if, in a few important ways, he tried to do what he imagined his late wife would have done, had she been alive.

My mother took a breath and allowed herself to be transported back to the earlier, happier part of that evening. "Hugh and I were in different colleges by then, but he still spent his summers with us. He had a job teaching sailing at Busman's Harbor Yacht Club. There was a tent on the old croquet lawn, and a live band. It was a perfect August night. Bright stars, light breeze."

I closed my eyes and pictured Morrow Island

before the buildings that housed the Snowden Family Clambake were built, when the great lawn was an expansive plateau below the stone staircase that led up to Windsholme.

My mother continued. "Your father was there. So handsome. We were so in love."

This part of the story, I did know. It was the stuff of family legend, how the lonely girl, a summer resident on a private island, had fallen in love with the boy who delivered groceries on his skiff, who had fallen for her too. And how they clung together, despite family objections, despite separations, and despite the odds against all summer romances. They'd married, raised a family, founded a successful business, and stayed in love until my father's death from cancer six years earlier. My mother was in love with him still.

"At first, no one noticed Hugh was missing." Mom's voice grew quieter and I sat forward on the chair, straining to hear. "My father had hired the *Morgana* to bring the guests out to Morrow Island, and take them and the caterers and the musicians home when the party was over. Some people came in their own boats, but most sailed on the *Morgana*. I kissed your dad good-bye, maybe a little too passionately for public consumption, but I was so happy and so in love. My father and I walked back to the house together. I expected to find Hugh there, but he wasn't. I waited up for him, thinking he was somewhere on the island, maybe with a girl, though I hadn't seen him with anyone in particular that night.

Hugh had been his usual gregarious, friendly self. Dancing with everyone. Telling jokes. The life of the party."

Mom gulped air and finished the story. "At dawn, when Hugh still wasn't home, Dad called the Coast Guard and we began to search. The obvious places at first—Windsholme, the play-house, the beach. By then, several friends had arrived from the mainland; we searched the whole island, climbing the bluffs, calling his name. Looking below . . ."

Her voice caught, and I mentally finished the sentence . . . *for a body on the rocks.*

"His body was never found," I confirmed. Sadly, that wasn't unusual given the ocean cur-rents in our part of the world. Lots of families in Busman's Harbor left flowers on graves where no body rested.

"No. And no one had seen him go to the mainland on the *Morgana.* And most telling, of course, he was never seen or heard from again."

"When did you last see him that night?"

"At ten, in the tent when they brought out the cake and the band played 'Happy Birthday.' He led the singing, as he did every year on my birthday, though it was usually just him and me and my dad, not a whole grand party."

"Was he drunk?"

"No. I'm sure he wasn't. His parents were both heavy drinkers. He hated that about them. He never overdid it."

"Other substances?" It was the seventies.

"I can't swear, of course, but I highly doubt it.

I knew him well. We'd been to lots of parties together. I'd never known him to take anything."

"Was he depressed?"

"Not that I could tell. To all outward signs, for most of his life, Hugh was the happiest, most well-adjusted person I knew."

"For most of his life?"

"There was something bugging Hugh that summer. I can't really describe it, but he was pensive. He often went off to other places on the island to be alone, which was unlike him. He was the definition of a people person."

"Did you ask him about it?"

"I tried, but he refused to open up. Said it was nothing." She paused. "After two days, the Coast Guard called off the search. Morrow Island is so tiny. We'd explored every nook and cranny of it. Seven years later, my father told me that Hugh's parents had him declared dead."

"His parents didn't tell you this personally? Seven years later you were a wife and mother, not a young girl to be shielded. You had been Hugh's best friend."

"I never had a relationship with Hugh's parents. My father barely did."

"They didn't come to Maine at all, during the search or after?" I couldn't imagine any parent who wouldn't rush to the place where their son was last seen to help search for him. What kind of people were they? It seemed beyond cold, almost pathological.

"No. My father went to the mainland to call them on the phone that first day. After that, they kept up communications with the Coast Guard, which was easier." Communicating with Morrow Island had been only by radio then, as it still was today. "They never expressed any interest in coming east."

"Do you know if either of his parents is still alive?"

She shook her head. "No idea. They'd be quite old, I think. Older than my dad."

We stared into the dying fire. Hugh had been the one who knew about the Black Widow. He'd been the only relative my mother knew, so he'd seemed like the best route to an answer. But my mother truly believed that was a dead end. I'd have to figure something else out in the morning.

Chapter 6

I woke up the next morning to the sound of the town plow. I'd heard it go by a few times in the night, but in the daylight something had changed. I lay in the warmth of my childhood bed, listening. What was it?

Silence. The wind no longer howled. Once the plow had continued up the road and out of earshot, there was nothing to hear. The sun streamed through the windows. I reached up and turned the light switch. Still no power. Not surprising. It often took a while for Maine Power to get to us.

My phone said 6:54. More important, it said it was at 20 percent power. I shut it off in case I needed it later. I heaved myself out of the warm bed and dressed in as many layers as I could scare up from the discarded bits of wardrobe still stored in my old room. The house was cold. The heating system was oil, but the pilot light required electricity. Hot water required electricity too. A shower would have to wait for later.

Mom was already in the kitchen, brewing coffee on the stove using an old camp pot she kept stowed in the pantry for just these occasions.

"Morning."

"Morning. Sleep well?"

"Yup. You?"

I gazed out the window into the backyard, a sun-dazzled, white wilderness. Somewhere under all that stuff was our driveway. I sighed. It would have to be dug out.

When I'd finished my coffee, I put on more layers and made for the front door, the shortest route to the street. "I need to go check on Le Roi," I called to Mom. "Back in a jiff."

"Bring him back with you. It'll be cold in your apartment. We'll light the fireplace here."

Outside, my L. L. Bean boots sunk into the snow, but the sun felt great on my face. According to the thermometer on the front porch, the temperature was in the upper thirties. At least we didn't have to worry about the pipes freezing while the heat was out.

The town stirred slowly to life. A pickup drove by me as I walked in the street. Then a Subaru. I was acutely aware of the Black Widow sitting back in the safe at Mom's house. It was extremely weird walking around being one of only two people—or three if you counted Mr. Gordon—or four if you counted whoever sent it—who knew there was something possibly worth two million dollars at Mom's house.

How could I find out where the necklace came from, or who might have a better claim to it than us? The web was out until the power came back on. The library was probably closed due to the power outage. But then I realized one place was sure to be open. The Busman's Harbor Historical Society. It would be open because the woman who ran it, Mrs. Floradale Thayer, lived above it.

At my apartment, I grabbed Le Roi's food and dug the cat carrier out from the storage closet under the eaves. The moment he saw it, Le Roi preened and pranced. In the harbor, the carrier could only mean one thing; he was being transported to car-free, predator-free Morrow Island. There he ruled all he surveyed from the top of his particular food chain, and kind-hearted seniors and little children snuck him lobster meat under their tables.

He jumped in. I closed the lid. "Boy, are you in for a surprise," I told him. "Life is full of disappointments."

I clumped him back to Mom's house. He weighed close to thirty pounds, so it wasn't easy. When I came over the hill, I heard a scraping sound and saw Sonny in his pickup, plowing Mom's driveway. Thank goodness. He usually plowed Mom out after a big snow, but I hadn't been sure if he'd risk traveling twenty minutes away from Livvie with her due date so close. I waved and called out a thank-you as he backed out of Mom's drive and started on the Snugg sisters' across the street. When I reached Mom's door, Viola Snugg came out on her front porch stamping her feet. She wore high-heeled boots, trimmed with a strip of lamb's wool around the ankles. Terribly impractical for a woman in her middle seventies out in a Maine winter, but Vee was always glamorous. I'd never seen her, at any time of day, without her white hair swept up in a chignon and full makeup on her strangely unlined face.

"Julia! I had stew meat in the fridge, and with the power out, I have to cook it all. You come over for dinner tonight with your Mom. You too, Sonny! Bring Livvie and Page."

Sonny put the truck in park and called back, "Okay. If Livvie's not in labor, we'll be there."

I was surprised he agreed. In the harbor, we were about seven minutes farther from the hospital than he and Livvie were at home. The cabin fever in their house must be considerable.

By the time I left for the Busman's Harbor Historical Society, around ten, the town was awake and bustling. There was still no power, but on Main Street, Gleason's Hardware had its door propped open and was selling ice melt and whatever other goods the snowed-in and power-less might need, for cash or on account, since the credit card machine wasn't working.

At the historical society, I was pleased to see the short front walk was neatly shoveled. Mrs. Thayer was home and open for business. The society occupied the first floor of a brick house with black shutters and a brass sign that told me it was built by the Lewis family in 1840. Floradale Lewis Thayer was one of their descendants. It was the only brick house on the town common. Though a few other houses were equally grand, they were built of wood.

I knocked, feeling a bit like Dorothy calling on the Wizard.

Mrs. Thayer threw open the heavy door. "Julia Snowden! I knew you'd turn up here sooner or later."

Did she know about the necklace?

"Why do you say that, Mrs. Thayer?" She was a big woman. Enormous, in fact. Well over six feet with the shoulders of a linebacker and, despite her sixty-plus years, the posture of a U.S. Marine. She'd always intimidated me.

"Because you Morrows have such a rich history in the town. I knew one of you was bound to take an interest, and when I heard you'd moved back, I knew it would be you."

I was at a loss as to why she thought this. I had met Mrs. Thayer maybe a dozen times in my adulthood. How could she have formed any impression of me? I was pretty sure I'd never mentioned any interest in my family's forebearers. "As a matter of fact, that's why I'm here."

"Then let's get started." Mrs. Thayer hustled me through the living room, which, like the dining room across the hallway, held the society's exhibits—old furniture, flags, and quilts, anchors and ship's figureheads, along with an ever-changing display of black and white photos.

In a back room crowded with bookshelves and file cabinets, she sat me at a large oak table. "Where shall we start?" she asked.

I wanted to know about two things, the Black Widow and my mother's family tree— specifically, who was around who might have sent the necklace or who might have a claim to it. I was reluctant to say this to Mrs. Thayer directly. Instead I answered more generally, "I'd like to know about my mother's family."

"I have just the thing." It was widely known around town that Mrs. Thayer ran the historical society with an iron hand. The society was a nonprofit, with a board, supposedly. But it was in Floradale's house and was composed of items and archives she'd assembled over decades, so she did what she wanted, and the board members, if they had any contrary opinions, kept them to themselves.

Mrs. Thayer completely rejected computers, which seemed like an odd thing for a person, much less an organization, devoted to history and genealogy to do. But she had tried personal computing once, in the 1980s, the story went, hadn't liked the experience and wasn't going to try it again.

On this particular day, I was grateful for her dislike of technology. The power was still out. Sun shone through the wavy glass of the old house's back windows, providing some heat, but not enough, which explained why Mrs. Thayer wore an overcoat, scarf, and fingerless gloves.

She went to a card file. "Morrow, Morrow,

Morrow," she muttered, rifling the cards. She pulled one out, stalked to a cabinet, and pulled out a file. "Let's start here." She put the file in front of me.

Inside was a photo of an oil painting, the portrait of a man with a long face and a long nose. He had on a high, stiff collar, and a black cravat at his throat. The man wasn't wearing a wig, so the portrait must have been painted after that particular fashion trend had ended, but not much, I didn't think.

"That's Frederic Morrow." Mrs. Thayer's voice rang with weighty import. "He started it all."

I was staring into the face of the original progenitor. "He started the family?" I asked. "In America?"

"No, he wasn't the first Morrow to come here. He was born in New England, on a farm outside Boston. He's the man who founded the family business and made the original fortune." As she talked, Mrs. Thayer moved back and forth between two additional card files, peering into each through her reading half-glasses. She bustled over to a bookshelf, plucked off a thick book, and put it down in front of me. *A History of the Morrow Ice Company*, it said on the beige cover, which was encased in plastic like a library book. "Your family made their money in the frozen-water trade. They sold ice."

"To the Eskimos?" I made the obvious joke.

"To the English in the Bahamas and India, to the Spanish in Havana, and to the French in

Haiti. The English in England never took to ice, but not for want of Frederic trying." She sniffed. "They still drink their beer warm, I'm told." She pointed to the book. "Frederic Morrow was the man with the vision to see what no one else did. Before him, ice was a small, personal operation. If you had a farm pond, and you lived in a place where water froze, you cut the ice on the pond and stored it in your icehouse, which was built into the ground. You used it to preserve food and for iced drinks and desserts in the summer. But Frederic Morrow understood the value people in hot places would put on ice." She cleared her throat. "Seeing you don't seem to know a thing about it, perhaps you'd best start reading."

I was intrigued, to say the least, to have this door suddenly opened to my ancestors. Mom had never mentioned the Morrow Ice Company. It was probably one more thing she'd lost when her mother died so young.

I looked at the man with the long face and the long nose again. *If not for you, I would not be here. I would not be me.* Under Mrs. Thayer's ever-watchful eye, I turned to the first page of the introduction to *A History of the Morrow Ice Company* and started to read. The book was written in the 1950s by a well-credentialed professor at the Harvard Business School, where Frederic Morrow's business diaries resided.

The story of the first man who loaded ice, packed in hay, on tiny wooden ships and sent it halfway around the world was fascinating. However, I still had a two-million-dollar necklace sitting at home in our safe. That little problem generated a lot of urgency. Interested as I was, I needed to move on.

When Mrs. Thayer finally drifted back to her desk, I used the opportunity to skip ahead in the book, turning to the first section of photos, which were on glossy pages about a third of the way through. The photos were reproductions of painted portraits of men, always men, including the one I had already seen of Frederic Morrow. There was also a reproduction of a woodcut print of men and horses on a frozen pond, cutting the thick ice into enormous strips, using a tool that looked like a cross between a plow and a sled.

The images in the second section of plates were newer, all photographs by then—men in muttonchops and icehouses in exotic locations. It was finally in the third set of plates, the ones from the 1890s through the 1920s, that I found was I was looking for, a photo of a formidable woman dressed in Victorian garb, wearing the Black Widow. My mother was right. The necklace had been ours. My heart pounded, pulsing blood that echoed in my ears.

"That's Sarah Morrow." I'd been so transfixed by the photo, I hadn't heard Mrs. Thayer come up behind me. "And that"—she pointed at the necklace's center stone—"is a seventy-carat black diamond."

"Holy cow." I knew what it was. I had seen it in real life, but the idea still bowled me over.

"Your three-times great-grandfather, Lemuel Morrow, gave that to her. The diamond was a celebration of the triumph of his business. Black diamonds are sometimes called 'black ice,' and in his business, black ice was considered the best ice of all. Black meant the ice was perfect, frozen quickly with no air bubbles. Black ice stayed frozen longer and was more aesthetically pleasing to the customers."

"I wonder what happened to the necklace," I ventured.

"No one knows," Mrs. Thayer snapped, in a tone that implied if she didn't, no one did.

Chapter 7

"Let me get this straight," Sonny protested. "Your relatives made their money selling frozen water? Un-freaking-believable."

We were gathered around the Snugg sisters' formal dining table, eating beef stew out of china soup bowls. Its aroma filled the room, mingling with the smell of burning wood and candle wax. The power hadn't returned, but the fire in the hearth threw heat and light across the oriental carpet. The silver candelabra on the table supplied the rest of the light.

"He *was* unbelievable," I countered. "He was the only person who believed ice would last long enough to be shipped so far. He spent years looking for investors, went to debtor's prison twice." New England had no cash crop like cotton or tobacco, no natural resources like iron or coal. Ships came into its ports filled with goods from Europe and departed with boulders in their hulls to provide the needed ballast. Frederic Morrow had seen an opportunity.

"He had to build icehouses in Havana, Port-au-Prince, Madras, everywhere he shipped the ice." My words came out in a rush. "When he first sold ice in Cuba, a customer took it home and left it on his front steps, then complained that he'd been sold a faulty product when it disappeared. So Frederic invented a device to store ice in the home. Then he figured out he could leave a little ice in the hulls of his ships for the return trip and bring tropical fruits and vegetables to New England," I concluded, with a flourish. "One man invented three industries, ice exporting, the home icebox, and frozen food. And he is our ancestor."

"They made enough money selling ice to build Windsholme?" Page asked. Her idea of buying ice was probably the chest outside the gas station where we picked up extra cubes for parties.

"Yes," I answered. Her amber eyes widened. Frederic Morrow had died at the age of eighty-one, in 1864. Windsholme wasn't built until 1890. His descendants had grown the family fortune even larger, but I didn't know who had done it or how. I'd only managed to read four chapters of *A History of the Morrow Ice Company*. I'd known better than to ask Mrs. Thayer if I could borrow the book. None of her painstakingly assembled collection was ever lent. I'd taken down the information and would search for the book on the web when the power came back on.

"*Where* did all this happen?" Livvie asked.

It was a reasonable question. My mother had grown up in New York City, where her father taught at Columbia. Hugh's family had lived in San Francisco. There was no obvious family seat. "In Boston," I answered. "Frederic started his business cutting ice on the ponds around Boston, and then loaded the big blocks onto horse-drawn carriages that hauled them over barely passable roads to the port. Later, he built railroads to bring the ice to the harbor. Henry David Thoreau woke up the middle of the night at Walden to see sixty men with horses on Walden Pond harvesting the ice. He hated the noise and the industrial nature of the operation, but even he couldn't escape the romanticism of knowing water he had bathed in would end up in India."

"The ice business may have started out in Boston," Fee Snugg said, peering through her thick glasses, "but the best ice in the world was cut right here in Maine on the Kennebec River. There were icehouses all up and down the river back in its day." Fee was as plain as her sister Vee was glamorous. She liked people well enough, though her great love was her succession of Scottish terriers. The latest, Mackie, slept in front of the fire.

The conversation flowed around me—tidbits about the history of the town, a discussion about whether the ice froze earlier and thicker back then than it did today. I dug into Vee's beef stew. I'd had it many times before, but this batch seemed especially good. The beef was flavorful and tender, the vegetables soft enough to spear with a fork, but not so soft they fell apart. The familiar dish warmed and comforted me, as did the company. I caught Mom's eye across the table in the candlelight and lifted a glass of the Snugg sisters' excellent Malbec to toast our secret.

Then Livvie asked me the obvious question. "Why all this sudden interest in our ancestors' business?"

I hadn't told them about the necklace. This was my sister, her husband, her child, and two of our family's most trusted, oldest, closest friends. Why did I hold back? Mom had said nothing about the Black Widow. It was her secret to tell, so I followed her lead. "I have time this week with the restaurant closed and I've always been interested."

"You have?" Livvie sounded skeptical, but she let it pass.

When the meal was finished, I stood to clear the table. I was as comfortable in Fee and Vee's kitchen as I was in Mom's or my own. I thought Livvie might follow and we'd have a chance to talk, but as she rose, everyone told her to stay put and relax.

"Enjoy the last weeks of your pregnancy," Mom said. "You'll be busy soon enough."

Sonny and Page and I did the dishes. I loved watching them together, two heads of fiery red hair bent to the task. When we were almost done, Mom stuck her head through the swinging kitchen door. "Sonny and Page, can you finish up? I need to take Julia and Livvie across the street for few minutes."

Sonny furrowed his red eyebrows, but when Page grumbled, "Probably baby stuff," his face smoothed out.

Poor Page. She was a typical oldest-only, comfortable with adults, maybe more than with her peers. The cozy world she'd occupied as the beloved single focus of two devoted parents was about to come to a screeching halt. I thought her disdain for the "baby stuff" was a cover for her anxiety. She had no way to imagine what was to come.

We were out into the street, bundled up against the bracing night air. The full moon lighting the snow made up for the darkened streetlamps. Mom and I walked on either side of Livvie, holding her arms to make sure she didn't slip in the road. Livvie, normally grace personified, had turned ungainly in her last month of pregnancy.

"What is this about?" she demanded.

"There's something you need to see," Mom answered.

We climbed the front steps and stomped our boots across the porch. When we got inside, Livvie tried again. "What the heck is going on?"

Mom took a flashlight out of her coat pocket and we felt our way upstairs to the clambake office. She trained the light on the safe while I twirled the combination. I could sense Livvie's tension. "It's nothing bad," I reassured her. At least I hoped it wasn't.

I opened the safe and took out the white jewelry box. Mom and Livvie gathered close as I pulled off the lid with a flourish.

"It's a box of cotton?"

Darn, I'd forgotten about the padding. I removed the top layer of cotton and the Black Widow sat on its downy white bed, caught in the stream from Mom's flashlight.

"What is it?" Livvie asked. With its enormous black gem and Victorian design, the necklace looked like costume jewelry.

"It's the Black Widow," Mom said. "It belonged to my great-great-grandmother."

"Someone sent it to Mom anonymously," I added. Livvie was silent, still not getting why we'd pulled her out of Fee and Vee's warm house to see this. I took the necklace out of the box, dangling it from my fingers while Mom shone the flashlight on it. The big black diamond sparkled like a Christmas ornament. "It's real," I said. "Mr. Gordon thinks it might be worth two million dollars."

In the dark room, I heard Livvie's sharp intake of breath, but no intelligible words followed.

I walked Livvie out to the pickup, which Sonny had idling in the middle of the street. She hadn't recovered from her initial shock, or asked nearly as many questions as I'd expected. Even though I'd passed along Cuthie Cuthbertson's cautions and caveats, it appeared Livvie was as bowled over by the idea of two million dollars as I had been when I first heard those words.

As their truck chugged away, I pulled my cell phone from the pocket of my down coat and turned it on. Two calls from Chris, one this afternoon, one twenty minutes ago. Holding the phone in my slippery wool gloves, I called him back.

"Hello, beautiful."

"Hello! Where are you?"

"In port. Key West. Got in today."

Relief flooded through me. Parts of my body I hadn't even realized were tense relaxed. When Chris was off in a little boat on a big sea, I tried not to think about it. I told myself he was an expert, as were Joe and Sam. But I'd almost lost him in a boating accident in the fall and worry was never far. "How is it down there?"

"Beautiful. Warm. I'm barefoot right now."

"Don't tease me."

"Truly. Coming across, the sunsets over the Caribbean were incredible, and the stars at night. We have to do this sometime. Together."

"Sounds wonderful. When will you be home?"

"Saturday. Joe's got a week to get this boat shipshape before the tourists start showing up for their excursions, and I want to give him a hand. Sam's going to stay longer, but I'll come back so we can resupply and open the restaurant on Monday. A ticket to Portland was crazy expensive, so I'm flying into Boston. I'll take the train up."

"Great. I'll pick you up at the train station in Portland. Can't wait."

I was surprised to realize that I couldn't wait. I'd been single for years when I'd lived in New York, and I'd thought I would relish a little alone time, a break from the man I worked with and all but lived with. But it turned out, I didn't need a break at all. I wanted him home.

"What have you been up to?" he asked.

"You won't believe it. Someone sent my mother a diamond necklace in the mail. Anonymously."

"A diamond necklace?"

"It's a family heirloom. I've been tracking down relatives." As quickly as possible, I told him what I'd learned.

"So your family made their money in the frozen-water trade?"

"Crazy, huh?"

His voice dropped, echoing concern. "Who have you told this to?"

"Just family so far. And the Snugg sisters. Why?"

"Julia, the ice business in Maine was brutal and dangerous. I had ancestors who worked the rivers, back in the day. Men and horses regularly broke through the ice and drowned. Or got caught in the machinery that carried the ice from the river to the icehouse. Many of the workers were children. They were old men by the time I was growing up, but I remember the stories. People in Maine regarded the ice barons the way people in Pennsylvania and West Virginia regarded the coal barons—as ruthless men who exploited people and natural resources. The ice barons were seen as worse than the coal barons, since they didn't even own the rivers they took the ice from. It was like making money off public property."

"Oh." I'd seen Frederic Morrow as creative and entrepreneurial, a genius inventor. I hadn't stopped to consider this side of the story.

"I wouldn't go mouthing around about your relatives making piles of money from the ice trade and buying two-million-dollar diamond necklaces," Chris concluded. "People in Maine have long memories."

At the end of the call, I stood in the dark road. People in Maine did have long memories. Even though my family had forgotten their past, that didn't mean everyone else had.

The streetlights flickered on. I looked at Mom's house. A warm light glowed in through the clambake office window. The power was back.

Chapter 8

My phone buzzed on the bedside table. I'd spent the night at Mom's. By the time the power came back, it had felt too late to pack up Le Roi and slog over the hill to my apartment.

Livvie. "Julia! I've done nothing all night but think about that necklace."

"It's a mystery," I agreed.

"Not the necklace. The money," she clarified. "Think about what we can do with it. We can pay off Quentin, for starters."

I rolled onto my stomach, balanced on my elbows, and held the phone out in front of me. "I know." The truth was, I had thought a lot about the money too. "The necklace may not even be ours," I cautioned. "Remember, Cuthie says these cases are almost always a mess. Other people who think they have claims 'will crawl out of the woodwork.' That's a quote."

"What other people?"

"That's what I'm trying to figure out."

"The note says 'For Windsholme,'" Livvie said. "So it must be from someone who knows about us. I think it means we're supposed to fix up Windsholme."

"Or it could mean 'This is a remembrance of Windsholme,' or 'This is to atone from something that happened at Windsholme,'" I suggested.

"I don't like the sound of that."

"No."

At the moment Windsholme was boarded up against the elements, awaiting a decision about its fate, though deep down, all of us knew fixing it up would never make economic sense. We were putting off the inevitable, horrible decision to tear it down.

"Even if the Black Widow is Mom's," I said, "she won't get all the money. There may be gift or estate taxes to pay, and the auction house will get a big cut. We'll have to spend money to have the necklace authenticated and insured. Plus, we'll probably have to pay lawyers a bunch to prove we own it."

Livvie sighed. "And I was in such a good mood."

"Did you tell Sonny about it?"

"Of course." She and Sonny had been together for so long, they practically shared a brain.

"What does he think?"

"Same as you. Don't get my hopes up. What does Chris say?"

"That the people who made money on ice exploited the workers and rivers of Maine."

"Figures. That's what you get for dating a commie."

I laughed. "So says another member of the proletariat."

"Ah, but I have ambitions not to be. Figure out who the necklace belongs to, will you? We need to either get this money, or I need to stop dreaming about it."

Mom had already taken off for work. I took advantage of her hot water heater for a long shower, enjoyed a cup of coffee in the kitchen, and then gathered Le Roi and his food for the trek back to my apartment.

The cat was already loaded into his carrier when a familiar clanging rang out from somewhere deep in the house. The landline. I set Le Roi down and headed toward the sound. The phone in the kitchen was so ancient, it didn't have a display to show me who was calling.

I picked up. "Hello?" Silence. Or maybe breathing. I pressed the old receiver to my ear, trying to tell which it was. "Hello. Who's calling?" More silence. I tried one more time. "Hello?"

There was a click and a dial tone.

I stood in the kitchen, fully dressed to go outdoors, my heart beating. Wrong numbers happened all the time, but everyday occurrences seemed different and more sinister with a two-million-dollar necklace in the house.

In the front hall, I upended Le Roi's case. He threw me a quizzical look. "Sorry, old man.

We'll be staying with Mom tonight." The phone call had unnerved me enough I didn't want to leave Mom alone in the house with the Black Widow. Tomorrow, before her shift started, I'd take her to First Busman's Bank to rent a safe deposit box.

I removed several layers of outerwear and climbed the stairs to the office. At the computer, I started the simplest way I could think of, entering "Hugh Morrow" into a search engine. It was far too common a name to get anything useful. "Hugh Morrow" and "San Francisco" wasn't helpful either. Cousin Hugh had disappeared in 1978, so I added the date, hoping a San Francisco paper had covered the loss of a native son, but got only hits in our local paper. The articles confirmed the story my mother had told. A young man disappeared from a party, "a relative of the birthday celebrant." The man's friends and the Coast Guard carried on a fruitless search, which ended three days later. Thanks were issued on behalf of the family by my grandfather. As Mom had told me, Hugh's parents never talked to the press.

One thing in the article did stop me in my tracks—a photo of my father as a young man, walking across the craggy rocks of Morrow Island, his hands cupped around his mouth, no doubt calling Hugh's name. "John Snowden, a friend of the missing man, searching Morrow Island," the caption read. Seeing Dad, suddenly summoned up by the web, so young, so healthy, brought tears to my eyes. The futility of what he was doing made the photo even sadder.

I sighed and stretched, annoying Le Roi, who'd settled in my lap. Clearly, garden-variety web searching wasn't going to work. Had I really thought I could find someone who'd been missing for more than thirty-five years simply by Googling him?

I did successfully find Frederic Morrow, in Wikipedia, among other places. My ice-industry-inventing ancestor was famous. The site provided more information about his personal life than *A History of the Morrow Ice Company* had—at least the parts I'd been able to read. He'd married quite late in life, at almost sixty, his empire secure. Nonetheless he'd gone on to have eight children, four boys and four girls.

I got out my credit card and entered the number into a genealogy site on the web. I was going to have to build a bridge from Frederic to my mother and therefore to me.

I quickly abandoned that strategy as impossible. With seven generations between Frederic and me, he had hundreds, probably thousands of descendants. Lots of those descendants had already created family trees on the genealogy site, which made my searches fast, but not particularly fruitful. There was no way to find my way through the thicket of people descended from Frederic Morrow to my own branch of the family tree. Besides, Morrow Island hadn't been purchased until 1880, ten years before Windsholme was completed, and the Black

Widow hadn't come into the family until around that time, either. Everyone who was out of the direct line before 1880 was irrelevant to my search.

Flexing my fingers, I started back the other way, working from what I knew. I knew my mother's name, Jacqueline Fields, and date of birth. I knew her mother's maiden name, Ellen Morrow. From there I got to my great-grandparents' names. Like my mother, they had lived in New York City. But my great-grandfather, born in 1905, was still two generations younger than the purchaser of Windsholme and the Black Widow. I had to keep looking.

There weren't any helpful family trees constructed by other people along this path. Why would there be? My mother and her mother were both only children. Who else would be looking?

I placed Le Roi, protesting rigorously, on the floor and went downstairs to the kitchen. I made myself a tuna sandwich and returned to my desk. Momentarily stymied in my investigation up my mother's line, I searched the genealogy site for information about Hugh. In its richer database, I was able to locate his death certificate; 1985, seven years after his disappearance, as my mother had said. His parents must have petitioned the court to have him declared deceased as soon as the law allowed it.

The death certificate gave me his parents' names, something I surely could have asked my mother for, which in turn gave me access to their listing in the San Francisco city directories of the 1980s. I opened another browser and found a street view of their home, an imposing brick mansion on Divisadero Street. There was obviously still plenty of money in Hugh's family in the eighties. I thought of the modest New York City apartment where my mother had grown up. Yet she was the one who owned Morrow Island. Funny how families evolved.

I searched through documents associated with Hugh's father, mostly city listings affirming he remained at the Divisadero address. I'd resigned myself to not finding anything useful and was burrowing down rat holes in a vast world of data, when something did come up. A birth certificate. Not for Hugh, but for an Arthur Morrow, thirteen years Hugh's senior. Hugh Morrow had a brother. Why hadn't Mom told me about him? Perhaps the family had gone on.

Chapter 9

Half an hour later, stiff from sitting and eyes vibrating with fatigue from staring at the screen, I pulled on my coat and boots and walked over the hill toward the Busman's Harbor Historical Society. My initial attempts to find Arthur Morrow on the genealogy site and on the web had come to nothing, but I was still buoyed by optimism. Hugh's branch of the family had come down to my mother's generation, which meant Arthur, or one of his kids or grandkids, might have sent Mom the Black Widow. But why? And how might they have ended up with it in the first place? I was determined to spend a few more hours with *A History of the Morrow Ice Company*, and whatever else Floradale Thayer had to offer.

Unlike the day before, the town common was alive with children, sledding, screaming, and throwing snowballs. The sunny sky and warmer temperature had brought them out. I spotted

Page waiting her turn at the top of the common's small hill, an old blue plastic sled in her hands. She returned my wave with a modest gesture intended not to attract the attention of her friends.

When I knocked on the historical society's front door, Mrs. Thayer's swift footsteps echoed from the back of the house. "I thought you'd be back," she said, peering down at me from her great height. She turned and walked away. I followed.

She had papers spread out across the oak conference table where I'd worked the day before. I'd interrupted her in the middle of a project. She pointed toward a small desk in the corner. I removed my coat, hung it on a wooden coat-rack, and sat on the hard chair.

"And today?" Mrs. Thayer asked.

"I'd like to see *A History of the Morrow Ice Company* again. And anything else you think might be useful."

Mrs. Thayer retrieved the book from the shelf. "Start with this. I'm in the middle of something. I'll bring more items when I'm done."

I skimmed through the middle chapters of the book, which chronicled the building of ice-houses, the purchase of ships, and the vagaries of New England winters—years when the ice was clear and clean and three feet thick, and years when the ice came late and melted early. Over the course of the nineteenth century, the business had moved north, from the lakes and ponds of Massachusetts to the great rivers of Maine.

The ice harvesters worked at night, when the temperatures were lowest. An engraving captured shadowy images of the river, teeming with men, boys, and horses in the darkness.

At last, I came to the part of the book that covered the period between the Civil War and the new century, the time when Windsholme was built and the Black Widow acquired. I turned the pages eagerly. The Morrow who ran the ice company then was named Lemuel. His portrait showed a portly man with muttonchops and a waistcoat. His thick-lipped mouth turned up slightly in a self-satisfied grin. The ice business had changed yet again. It was no longer necessary to ship ice to India or the Caribbean. New residents poured into the cities of America—country people who'd migrated from the farms, and immigrants from Europe. Far from the sources of fresh food and thirsty from hard, physical work, the city residents demanded ice. New York alone needed four million pounds of it a day. The money rolled into the Morrow Ice Company.

"Here you go." Mrs. Thayer put a folder in front of me.

In it was a single photo of Windsholme, with Lemuel, his family, servants, and even his dog arranged artfully on the front lawn. In the sepia image, the magnificence of the house took my breath away. Windsholme had been empty my entire life, provided with the minimum of maintenance to keep it standing. In the picture, I could see the house for what it was—an architectural beauty. Its strong, clean lines must have seemed odd or even off-putting in Victorian times, but it blended perfectly with the raw power of the island setting.

In the photograph, the imposing figure of Lemuel stood on the terraced lawn. From the portrait, I hadn't been able to see how tall he was. His height along with his girth made him a formidable figure.

"Do you know who these other people are?" I asked Mrs. Thayer.

"Not by name, but we can tell by their clothing." She pointed to a man dressed in work clothes, holding a hedge trimmer. "The gardener. Windsholme was famous for its formal gardens. The yacht captain. The butler." She pointed to each in turn. Then she focused on the women. "Lemuel's mother, certainly." The senior Mrs. Morrow was as stout as her son, but short statured. The facial resemblance was unmistakable.

"Sarah Morrow, Lemuel's wife," Floradale continued, pointing to a woman in a high-collared dress. "You've already seen her photo in the book." Lined up a bit away from Sarah were two housemaids and a woman in more formal clothes.

"Housekeeper?" I guessed.

Mrs. Thayer squinted at the image. "Nanny, I'd say."

So these were the ancestors who'd built Windsholme, these funny Victorians who escaped the humid, disease-ridden cities of the Northeast in the summer by building a home on a rock in the cold North Atlantic. Windsholme, with its enormous public rooms, was meant for entertaining a summer-long flow of houseguests, not as a cozy family home.

On the other side of the lawn in the photo were two little boys, maybe five and three, in stiff sailor outfits, standing on either side of a cart. The smaller boy looked shyly out from under his dark bangs, while the older one stared boldly at the camera. Behind them was a swath of lawn that stretched all the way to the playhouse that still stood today, a miniature of Windsholme. The area around it had long since gone to woods, and it was a shock to see it as originally intended.

Mrs. Thayer followed my gaze. "That's William and Charles, the Cain and Abel of Morrow Ice Company."

"You're not saying one of them killed the other?" The possibility of murderous progenitors had never occurred to me.

"No, but they hated one another, and between them, they killed Morrow Ice."

This was the part I'd been waiting for. "Which one am I descended from?"

"William, the older one."

I stared at the boy. Did I recognize anyone I knew in his face? My mother, Livvie, Page, or even myself? I didn't. He seemed far away, and not just in time.

"How did he and Charles destroy Morrow Ice?"

"The business was all about New York City and its enormous demand. Shipping ice successfully meant that the winning companies not only had to control the ice, they had to control the ships that hauled the ice, and the labor unions that controlled the stevedores who unloaded the ships. Morrow had to compete against the big companies that harvested ice on the upper Hudson. The Hudson River was dirtier than the Kennebec, but it was also much closer to the city. Some years the Hudson froze sooner and thicker, and some years the Kennebec did." Mrs. Thayer looked at me to see if I was following. I was. I'd been in business long enough to understand risk.

"William and Charles had quite different temperaments," she continued. "William was a big personality, like his father. A hunter and a fisherman, a man's man. Charles was shy and bookish. They say he was never so happy as the years he was at Harvard. Yet their father left the business to them fifty-fifty. He didn't appoint a successor, either during his lifetime or in his will.

"When Lemuel stepped away from running the business, in 1910, your great-great-grandfather, William, moved from Boston to New York City. He became friends with the mayor and the whole gang at Tammany Hall. He cultivated the union leadership and bribed them to unload his ships first and the competitions' slowly or not at all. He began buying up assets—ships, icehouses, and other ice companies in Maine—as fast as he could.

"His brother, Charles, moved to Maine to manage the ice cutting and shipping operations here. He preferred Maine to New York, but it's not clear that he understood William had maneuvered him neatly out of the center of the business."

Mrs. Thayer pulled *A History of the Morrow Ice Company* toward her. She opened to the plate with the portrait of the two brothers as grown men. William was huge, like his father, practically squeezing Charles out of the frame. Charles looked away from the lens, as if distracted by something happening behind the photographer.

"Then, in the winter of 1914, it happened," Mrs. Thayer continued. "The Hudson had a bad ice year. The Kennebec froze hard and early. William demanded that ice be cut three times over the winter. By the spring the ice was dangerously soft. Not one, but two teams of horses broke through, pulling the men down with them to a watery death. Charles refused to harvest more. William was furious, but by that time there was more than enough ice stored in the houses along the Kennebec's banks.

"In late spring, the ships began to arrive at the docks in New York Harbor. William saw to it that what little ice his Hudson River competitors had managed to ship wouldn't be unloaded.

And then, having created a grinding shortage, he jacked the price of ice sky high.

"The city went wild. The press and the public turned against Morrow Ice. The newspapers portrayed the price hike as a war on the poor. Even William's Tammany Hall associates couldn't protect him. He was arrested for price-fixing and thrown in jail. The shares of Morrow Ice tumbled until they were practically worthless. The company had no cash, and most of its assets, the ships and the icehouses, had been bought with money borrowed against the worthless stock. There was no way to repay it.

"William was released on bail and spent the summer before his trial at Windsholme. It was there that he and Charles had it out. Charles was angry that the company their illustrious ancestor Frederic had built had been turned to dust, but he was also terrified of the debt Morrow Ice had incurred, worried that he and his young family would lose everything.

"William agreed to buy Charles's shares in the company for one cent a piece. He also demanded, as a condition of the deal, that Charles sign over his half ownership of Morrow Island and Windsholme. Charles left town for San Francisco with only train fare for his family and a few hundred dollars to start a new life."

So that was the schism, and the beginning of the New York and San Francisco Morrows. "What happened after that?"

Mrs. Thayer shook her head. "William was convicted of price-fixing and spent seven months at Sing Sing. After he got out, he tried to rebuild the company one last time and nearly succeeded, but then came World War I and right after that modern refrigeration. Once ice could be manufactured in the cities, there was no reason to ship it long distances. William's life collapsed. Charles, on the other hand, eventually made a fortune in San Francisco. He bought a huge mansion out there. But before that, during the early twenties, he and William made some kind of peace and Charles and his children traveled to Windsholme every summer to spend time with William's family and Lemuel's widow, Clementine."

I drew my head up sharply. "But you said Lemuel's wife was named Sarah."

"Clementine was Lemuel's second wife. She was younger than either of his sons and outlived Lemuel by forty years. She was the hostess at Windsholme, and she kept it as a great house into the roaring twenties. She hosted glamorous parties there during Prohibition. I have a photo of her somewhere." Mrs. Thayer went through her routine with the card file and retrieved another photo.

"She's wearing the necklace!" I tamped down my enthusiasm and said more solemnly, "The one Lemuel's first wife wore."

Clementine was dark and exotic looking in a way none of the stolid Morrows were. She'd been quite young when the photo was taken. It was hard to judge ages in old photos, but early twenties, I thought. She wore the straight dress of a flapper, so different from the Victorian clothing worn by Lemuel's first wife, Sarah.

"It was during one of those wild parties at Windsholme that the necklace disappeared," Floradale said. "Clementine reported it to the police and put it around that a housemaid had stolen the necklace, but there was never an arrest and I don't think anyone in town believed her. All that is known is neither the San Francisco cousins nor Clementine returned after that, not once. Soon the whole party was over. The stock market crashed in twenty-nine and Windsholme was closed up. Its furniture, silver, china, and artwork were loaded onto boats and shipped out of here. No one knows to where." She looked at me expectantly, like I might be able to fill in the blanks.

I knew where a tiny bit of the treasure was. There was one set of a dozen crystal wineglasses in the corner cabinet in my mother's dining room. Three minor paintings that had been in my grandfather's apartment were now on the wall in Mom's living room. Other than that, I had no idea. I assumed it was all sold during the Depression.

When Mrs. Thayer saw I wasn't going to say anything, she continued. "Windsholme has been empty ever since. Well, until you burned it down last summer."

"I didn't burn it, and it didn't burn *down*," I protested.

She shrugged, as if to signal my tiny corrections didn't matter. Disposition of historic property was serious business to her. "Your great-grandparents made the boathouse into the little cottage and that's where your grandmother spent her childhood summers. And then your mother, and then you and Livvie."

I nodded and thanked her. We were finally back to the part of the story I already knew.

Chapter 10

The sun was rapidly disappearing when Mrs. Thayer pushed back her chair from the conference table and announced, "That's it for today." I'd continued reading *A History of the Morrow Ice Company*, which confirmed pretty much the story she had told me.

When Mrs. Thayer had gone to the powder room, I'd used my phone to sneak photos of the picture of the family at Windsholme and the one of Clementine Morrow wearing the Black Widow.

I felt gleefully optimistic. The necklace had disappeared on a weekend when the San Francisco relations had been at Windsholme. Hugh Morrow had a brother, Arthur. All roads led to San Francisco. I sensed we were close to a breakthrough.

The snow had melted during the day and turned to ice as the sun went down. I crunched along carefully, smiling when I saw the lights blazing from Mom's kitchen window. She was home. I had so much to tell her.

I burst through the ever-unlocked kitchen to be hit in the face by a smell from my childhood.

"Meat loaf?"

She nodded. "I thought I'd entice you with one of your favorites, so I stopped at Hannaford on the way home from work. You'll stay?"

"I'm going to sleep over," I said.

Mom turned from the stove, arching a curious eyebrow at me.

"You had a call on the landline today," I told her. "The person on the other end didn't say anything, but someone was there, I'm sure."

Mom was unimpressed. "Happens all the time."

"It doesn't happen all the time when there's a two-million-dollar necklace in the house."

"Don't be silly. No one even knows it's here."

"Mr. Gordon does," I reminded her.

"The most trustworthy man in town. You don't think it was him?"

No, I didn't. "The person who sent the necklace knows it's here."

"Yes, but if they didn't want me to have it, they wouldn't have sent it in the first place. I'm in no danger, Julia."

I dug in my heels. "I'm staying tonight, and tomorrow morning we'll take the necklace to the bank and rent a safety deposit box."

She sighed. "Okay, but it's in the safe upstairs. I don't know why you're insisting."

"Mom, you never lock your house and everyone in town knows it. Two strong people could carry that safe down the stairs and right out of the house. I don't want to argue."

"Suit yourself. Make a salad, will you?"

I decided not to talk about the day's discoveries until I had her full attention, so it wasn't until we sat down at the table that I told her what I'd learned. She listened attentively as I told her the history of the last years of the Morrow Ice Company and the rift between the families after the disappearance of the necklace.

"Does any of this sound familiar?" I took a taste of the meat loaf while she considered her answer. Its oniony, catsupy, mustardy flavors tasted like home and childhood and safety.

Mom shook her head, and then said, "Hugh may have told me some of this. He'd heard only vague stories about why the two branches of the family didn't get along. And Hugh was the one who told me about the Black Widow, I'm certain. But he never said his family actually had it. Or that he'd seen it. Maybe he knew more than he said, but I doubt it. Our relationship was about telling the truth and cutting through all that had gone on between our families in the past. It was an act of rebellion for Hugh to befriend me, one his parents didn't like. And then we became real friends. We were both alone. He was like a brother to me."

"But Hugh wasn't alone," I pointed out. "He

had a brother. Why didn't you tell me about Arthur? Don't you think Arthur must have sent the necklace?"

Mom was quiet for a moment. "Julia, Arthur couldn't have sent the necklace. He died before Hugh and I even met."

Darn. I'd been so sure I was onto something, creeping toward an answer. "What happened?" It was an unimaginable tragedy. The loss of two sons.

"He was much older than Hugh, thirteen years older. He drowned in a sailing accident in San Francisco Bay. Hugh's mother never got over it. I had the impression Arthur was the favored son, the apple of the parental eye. Hugh always felt like the unwanted afterthought, particularly after Arthur died. He left for prep school the next year."

Mom looked down at her long, beautiful fingers. Her simple wedding ring was still on her left hand. "I spent a long time being furious at Hugh's parents, two people I'd never met. Can you imagine having a son who is so reluctant to go home for school vacations that he adopts the family of a classmate, a distant relative, on the other side of the country? How awful people are. When Hugh was lost and his parents didn't come out to Maine, I was even angrier. I realize now I was really mad at Hugh, that he'd been careless and gotten himself killed. I was angry at the world, which had given me the gift of Hugh's company, and then stolen him from me. My anger had to land somewhere, so it landed on Hugh's parents. But when you were born a few years later, I understood the enormity of their loss, why they couldn't bear to come here."

We sat for a moment while I absorbed what she'd said. The breadth and depth of the tragedy that had befallen Hugh's parents, losing both their sons, was staggering.

The phone rang, startling us both.

I reached it first. "Julia? Sonny. It's on. We're headed to the hospital. We've got Page with us. Can you meet us there?"

We flew up the peninsula in Mom's car to Busman's Harbor Hospital, then made tracks to Labor and Delivery. Page was in the waiting room, brow furrowed with anxiety. Normally she was too old for hugs in public places, but she threw herself into my mother's arms. "Grandma!"

"I'm sure everything's fine, dear," my mother reassured her. "What's going on?"

"Dad's in the back getting Mom settled." Page pointed past a pair of swinging doors. "He said you'd be here."

"And so we are."

I asked the young man at the reception desk to let Livvie and Sonny know we were there. At least I could relieve any worry they felt about Page by sending word that Mom and I had arrived.

Mom and Page were seated on hard plastic chairs in the farthest corner of the waiting area when I returned to them. "What happened?" I asked.

Page shrugged her broad swimmer's shoulders. "Nothing much. Mom had some pains. Dad yelled, 'This is it! Let's go.' We all got in his truck and here we are."

I sat down next to them. None of us had thought to bring anything to pass the time. Then I remembered the photos on my phone. "When I was at the Busman's Harbor Historical Society today, I saw a picture of Windsholme just a year after it was built. Do you want to see it?" Mom and Page nodded eagerly. Any distraction in a storm. I pulled up the image and passed them the cell phone.

"Oooh," Page said. Even a child couldn't miss the power and grandeur that had been Windsholme. "Who are the people?"

I walked them through the cast of characters on the tiny screen, giving the same commentary Floradale Thayer had, though I left out her remark about Cain and Abel.

Mom had put on her reading glasses, and she reached for the phone, studying the faces. "My gracious, it was a beautiful house. Julia, can you print this and make me a copy? I would so love to have it."

I nodded yes and took back the phone.

Time dragged and my bottom hurt from the hard chair. Mom and Page were engaged in a cutthroat game of hangman. "Anybody want anything from the machines? Page, did you get dinner?"

The words were no sooner out of my mouth when Sonny came through the swinging doors. He was dressed in his regular jeans, plaid shirt, and down coat, no scrubs. Livvie appeared behind him, also fully dressed.

"False alarm," Sonny announced.

"Braxton Hicks contractions," Livvie confirmed.

"You're not going to have a baby that way," a nurse said from the reception desk, "at least not tonight."

Livvie sagged against Sonny. "I'm exhausted. I want to go home to bed."

My mother stood and touched Livvie's arm. "Maybe Page could stay over with me?"

"Please," Page pleaded.

Livvie wearily nodded her assent. She looked like she'd agree to anything to get out of there.

Page turned to me. "Can you stay over at Grandma's too, Aunt Julia?"

"Don't bother Julia," Sonny answered for me. "She's got too many things to do. Two million things, in fact."

"I was already staying at Grandma's," I assured Page. She rewarded me with an enormous smile.

Chapter 11

I awoke in the morning with the sun shining through the windows. Le Roi raised a lazy head out of the quilt and narrowed his eyes. Why was I stirring on such a cozy morning? he seemed to ask. The twin bed in my childhood room was uncomfortable for the two of us, but it had one advantage as far as Le Roi was concerned—no Chris. He and Chris operated in a world of détente, neither too sure about the other. I'd adopted Le Roi at the end of the summer. His former family was no longer able to care for him, and no one else had stepped forward. Things were still tentative between Chris and me at the time, so as far as Le Roi was concerned, he'd staked his claim first. His relationship to me was primary and Chris was the interloper.

In the quiet kitchen, I fixed a pot of coffee and made a couple of slices of toast with blueberry

jam. The house was silent. Neither Mom nor
Page stirred.

The first task of the morning, even before getting dressed, was to head back to the computer.
I signed on to the genealogy site. Thanks to Floradale Thayer, I had a whole lot more names than
I'd had the day before. I built branches of the family
tree from me to Mom all the way back to the
brothers William and Charles, and then to their
father, Lemuel.

When I added Lemuel's name, my heart beat
a little faster. Someone else had put him in his
or her family tree. That meant someone else
had trod this path, looking for ancestors. The
long line of only children was over. There was a
relative somewhere, who had done what I was
doing. A relative I needed to find.

I tracked back down Charles's line to Hugh
and Arthur, all living in San Francisco and apparently a dead end. But then I realized Mom
had also given me a clue. Arthur was dead, and
I knew approximately when he'd died. The genealogy site didn't offer up an obituary, but did
give me a death certificate with an exact date,
July 11, 1969. I jumped over to a search engine
and kept looking.

It came up right away. There were newspaper
articles about the tragedy. He'd been swept overboard during a sailing race. Unlike Hugh's
death, there were several witnesses including the
rest of the crew. A rescue was attempted, though
it failed. Arthur had been knocked unconscious
before he went over, and sank like stone.

I followed a link to the first obituary I spotted. Arthur was given his due as the oldest son of a Gold Coast family, a man who had graduated from Harvard undergrad and then Stanford Law. He had worked with his father at Morrow and Wakefield, the family law firm. Arthur had been an active sailor and racer. The final paragraph of the obituary noted those left behind, listing his parents, brother Hugh—and Arthur's wife and infant daughter! His wife was named Louise, his daughter was Rose. She was less than a year old when her father died.

I yelped when I saw it, and Le Roi periscoped his head up from his spot in the sun on the rug, protesting the interruption to his slumbers.

"Wake up, you lazy bones," I called to him. "Exciting things are happening."

I stretched, went to the bathroom, and then threw a sweater over my T-shirt and pajama pants. Now that I knew their names, finding Louise Morrow and then Rose Morrow in San Francisco city directories was easy. It looked like they'd resided with Arthur's parents for a couple of years after the accident and then struck out on their own. But they didn't go far. They moved to an address just a few blocks away.

I worried Louise would remarry and I'd lose the trail. Arthur was only twenty-six when he died and Louise likely was quite young as well. But she continued to show up, as did Rose. In fact, though Louise's trail drifted off in the mid-nineties, Rose Morrow continued on.

I found Rose's photo on the web site of a

San Francisco hospital. She was a physician, a neurosurgeon. She stared out of her official photograph, a woman in her late forties, strong and confident, with deep brown eyes, thick, wavy, brown hair. Rose Morrow was mixed race, certainly part African-American.

That took me aback momentarily, but then I thought, why wouldn't she be? She was born in 1968, not 1908, and Arthur Morrow was free to marry anyone he wanted, and apparently, he'd wanted Louise. I wondered how this had gone over with his parents. Hugh had told Mom his mother cared only about what other people thought. It was hard to imagine Arthur's marriage had been the toast of the Gold Coast set. But it appeared Louise and Rose had lived with the Morrows after Arthur died, so how bad could the relationship have been?

I had a cousin Rose, a third cousin, once removed, if I calculated right. Rose must have inherited or found the Black Widow. She must have been the one who searched the genealogy site and built the family tree to Lemuel and Sarah, our common forebearers. But why? If she'd inherited the Black Widow, why hadn't she kept it, or sold it?

I paced until at last Mom emerged from her room, showered and fully dressed. "Did Hugh ever mention a sister-in-law or a niece?"

She didn't answer right away, but went down the back stairs to the kitchen where she poured a cup of coffee and sat at the kitchen table. I followed like an eager terrier, nipping at her heels. Why was she avoiding the question?

"I'm sure Hugh didn't mention a niece," Mom finally said. "He didn't like to talk about Arthur. The subject was painful for him. Do you mean Arthur had a daughter?"

"He did and I've found her on the Internet. A real, honest to goodness, living relation."

Mom stared at the tabletop. She'd said her relationship with Hugh was based on honesty. My heart broke for her. This had to be a serious blow. Maybe more important, what else hadn't Hugh told her? Finally she said, "What will you do now?"

"I'll figure out how to get in touch."

"And ask a perfect stranger, 'You didn't, by the way, happen to send my mother a two-million-dollar necklace?'"

I laughed. "Maybe not right off. I'm headed to the post office to verify that the package came from San Francisco."

I dressed in snug layers—T-shirt, flannel shirt, coat, scarf, gloves—and then realized, like a three-year-old, I had to pee before I went out. So I undid most of it and then had to put it all on again while Le Roi sat at my feet and laughed. Or, at least I imagined he laughed.

The day was clear like the previous one, and enough above freezing that the melt continued. On my way to the post office, I stopped off at Tom's Business Center to have the photos of

Windsholme and Clementine Morrow enlarged and printed. Mom had seemed so taken with the one of Windsholme. Clementine, I wanted for my own purposes.

"Hi, Julia," Barbara Jean called from behind the counter as soon as I entered the post office. There was no line, but three people stood around the high table in the center of the room, sorting mail they'd taken from their boxes. In true Busman's manner, I knew all of them, and we greeted each other by name and remarked on the snow and the melt and speculated about when the next storm might be.

I handed Barbara Jean the wrapping paper from the package as soon as I reached the counter. She entered the numbers from the machine-generated stamp into her computer. "Got it." She spoke softly, as if we were in a hospital elevator or a confessional. I smiled at her encouragingly, knowing what was coming. "Your package originated in Boston."

"Boston!" Nothing in my research had led me to Boston. Frederic, the first Morrow iceman, had started there, but Lemuel had moved to New York City and Charles to San Francisco, and the two families had continued in those places.

"Back Bay, specifically," Barbara Jean added.

Darn. I was going to have to start over. "Anything else?"

"It was sent last Tuesday, if that's helpful."

Every little bit. I thanked her and trudged out into the snow.

Tom at the business center had printed the photos. "She sure is a beauty," he said, sliding them into an envelope. It wasn't until he said "Shame she burned," that I realized he meant Windsholme, and not Clementine Morrow or the necklace.

Mom and Page were in the kitchen baking ginger snaps, as Mom was taught by Helga, one of the housekeepers who had raised her and provided her sketchy domestic education. As I watched, Page combined the dry ingredients with the wet and stirred the mixture. When the dough rolled into a big ball, Mom covered the bowl with plastic wrap and put it in the fridge. It would be several more hours before the house filled with the smell of their gingery deliciousness.

"Have you talked to your Mom or Dad this morning?" I asked Page.

"Yup."

"Everything's fine," my mother elaborated for her. "Livvie is resting."

"Where have you been?" Page asked. "My dad said you had something important to do."

"Don't worry. I'm doing it." I poured coffee for Mom and me and we sat at the kitchen table.

I wasn't sure how much I wanted to say in front of Page, but I figured if I didn't mention the Black Widow, or its value, which was the type of thing that might easily slip out in conversation with her friends, the rest was okay. "The package didn't come from San Francisco," I told Mom. "It came from Boston. Do you have any idea of someone who might have sent it from there?"

Mom's mouth drooped in disappointment. "No idea at all," she answered. "You know more about the family than I do at this point. Hugh went to Harvard, as did Arthur, so that's a Boston connection. But other than that, I couldn't say." She paused. "What will you do now?"

"I don't know. I was so sure it was Rose who sent the package. I may try to call her or e-mail her anyway. I'm out of clues." Then I remembered the printed photograph of Windsholme and pulled it from my tote bag. "I have something for you," I said, hoping it would cheer Mom up.

"Oooh, let me see." Page slid over next to me.

I had to admit the quality of the photo wasn't great. It had been blown up from a photo of a photo taken with my phone. Windsholme loomed, but the figures on the porch and lawn were fuzzy, their faces a perturbing congregation of wavy, disconnected lines. Despite this, my mother studied them intensely.

"What's that?" Page pointed to a cart that stood between the two little boys.

"I imagine it's something they played with," I answered.

"No, I mean what's in it?"

"I don't see." But then I squinted and I did.

"I'll get a magnifying glass." Mom opened the kitchen junk drawer, pulled out a cheap magnifying glass, and returned to the table. "It's a baby!" Mom gasped. "Another relative."

The trail had opened up again.

"Is it a boy or a girl?" Page asked.

"No way to know, sweetie," Mom said. "It's far too small to see, and anyway, they dressed them pretty much the same in those days."

"Oh," Page said, losing interest.

"Do you want a brother or a sister?" Mom asked her.

"We're not finding out," Page answered, giving the party line.

"I know," Mom prodded, "but it's so close now. Tell us what you really want. I know you will love the baby no matter what, but what are you wishing for?"

Page hesitated, and then blurted, "A boy."

"Really?" That surprised me. I thought a ten-year-old girl would want a little sister to dress up and play with. "Why?" Less competition?

"This family needs boys," Page said matter-of-factly. "We don't have enough."

"What will you do now?" Mom asked me.

"Follow up. Find out who the baby was. Maybe his or her descendants stayed in Boston."

"Start at the historical society," Mom advised. "Floradale got you this far."

The sidewalk up to the historical society door had melted to wet pavement, a far cry from the way it had been on my first visit. Mrs. Thayer answered on the first knock. Her project was still spread out across the conference table, so I again sat at the small desk in the corner.

"What would you like this time?" Mrs. Thayer asked.

"*A History of the Morrow Ice Company*, again, please, and the photo you showed me yesterday of Windsholme." I hadn't brought the blown-up photos with me. I was afraid admitting I'd photographed them would get me banned for life. This would take some finesse.

She gave me the book and the file with the photo and returned to her work. I looked casually through the photos, stopping at the one of Windsholme. "May I have a magnifying glass, please?"

Mrs. Thayer grunted, rising to cross the room to her desk. "Think you see something?"

Perfect. I pointed to the cart. "I think there's a baby in there."

"I don't need a magnifying glass for that. That's Lemuel and Sarah's daughter, William and Charles's sister."

My hopes soared. "Do you know what happened to her?"

"She died at the age of six, in the same scarlet fever epidemic that killed her mother." Floradale studied my reaction. "What's the matter? I know it's sad, but it happened many years ago."

I decided to lay my cards on the table, at least partially. "I'm trying to track down some relatives for my mom. It's really just her, you know. Her mother died when she was so young. She doesn't know much about the family. I did find one person, Arthur Morrow's daughter, but she's on the West Coast."

Mrs. Thayer sat in the chair next to me and put a hand as big as a basketball player's over mine. "Your mother's had more than her share of bad fortune. But what about Clementine's daughter? I realize she was a half sibling, but she's been at Windsholme. She might love to connect with your mother."

Clementine had a daughter? Clementine, Lemuel's second wife, who had been photographed wearing the Black Widow? "Do you know anything about the daughter?"

"She was a pip, that one. Went off to fight in the Spanish Civil War, married a Spanish freedom fighter."

"Did she stay in Spain?"

"No, no. Brought him back to her mother's house in Boston, in the Back Bay. Her name is Morales. Marguerite Morales."

I calculated in my head. It was so confusing. Marguerite had to be three decades younger than her half brothers, but she must be quite old now, if she was even still alive. "Do you know if she had children?"

"I lost track of her. She never returned to Busman's Harbor." Floradale's tone made it clear that if your life didn't include Busman's Harbor, it wasn't worth knowing about.

I jumped up and grabbed my coat. "Thank you, thank you, Mrs. Thayer. I've got to run."

Chapter 12

I thought it would be harder to find Marguerite Morales on the web than it was. Knowing not only that she had lived in Boston, but in Back Bay, made it easier. Marguerite Morales had been active in the Garden Club of Back Bay, the Alliance Française, and the Boston Athenaeum. Entries on the web were slimmer for her in recent years. She had to be well into her nineties, but I found no obituary. I couldn't believe my luck. Was she still alive?

I tracked down her exact address on Marlborough Street in Back Bay. Almost all the homes around were condos, but there were no unit numbers at Marguerite's town house. Perhaps she owned the whole building. I was skimming through the information about her address available on the web, reading about building permits sought and real estate taxes paid, when I noticed something that took my breath away.

Marguerite co-owned the house with a Hugh M. Morales!

At first, I assumed he was a husband or a son, but I couldn't find any evidence of that. Hugh Morales was as present on the web as Marguerite was. He was a realtor. He ran in 10K races. He was on the board of the Massachusetts Audubon Society. I typed in my credit card number to access the *Boston Globe* archives and found him in a group photo at the start of a road race. Could it be? Could it possibly be? He was lean like the runner he was, sharp featured and gray haired. Mom had plenty of photos of her cousin Hugh, but they stopped when he disappeared when he was twenty-one. I squinted at the image. The man in the picture was the right age. I couldn't be sure, but my hopes rose.

Just as with Marguerite, the mentions of Hugh on the web were scarcer in the last few years than previously. There had been nothing in a couple of years. But again, I found no obituary. Would you have an obituary and a funeral for a man who was already dead? My hands shook as I powered off the computer. *What should I do?*

I called Cuthie Cuthbertson. "Hello, Julia dear. What can I do for you this fine day?"

"I think I found the person who might have sent Mom the . . . tiara. At the very least, I've found a relative in Boston we didn't know we had."

"Good for you, dear."

"What do I do now? Should you call her?"

He didn't answer right away. Then he said, "Remember I told you these kinds of cases, questions of ownership, are always giant messes? The last thing you need is to start things off with a call from an attorney, even one as tactful as me. And I don't think you should call or e-mail either. I think you need to go down to Boston and meet face to face. What's the worst that can happen? You meet a new relative. You can't make the situation any trickier than it already is."

I knew before I hung up what I would do. What I had always planned to do, probably. I called Chris.

"Hey, beautiful. What's up?" He sounded relaxed, like a man wearing sandals, not snow boots.

"I found someone who might have sent the necklace to Mom. She's a distant cousin who lives in Boston. I'm going to go down there for a couple of days to see if I can meet her."

He was silent for a moment. "Take my truck. You shouldn't drive your old beater to Boston, or even to Portland to catch the train. The truck is heavy and it's loaded up with sand in the back. There's more weather coming your way at the end of this week."

He was right about my car, a 1982 Caprice with a wonky heater and questionable windshield wipers. It was definitely not to be driven off the peninsula. "Okay. Thanks."

"Do me a favor, throw my coat in the truck. If you're still in Boston when I fly in, you can pick me up at the airport. Maybe we'll even spend the night in a nice hotel."

"Wow. I'm sold. How much is Joe paying you that you have cash to throw around on hotel rooms?"

"It's not wasted when I'm with my girl."

I hung up with a ridiculous grin on my face. Chris was a handsome man. Almost too handsome, as I was reminded as I walked around Busman's Harbor and women, so many women, stopped to inquire how he was and to reminisce about their time with him. He had a wonderful voice, strong and masculine, with a hint of a Maine accent that made me tingle whenever I heard it. And when he said things like that . . .

I returned to my apartment and packed a small bag. When I got back to Mom's house, she and Page were reading in the living room. "I'm going to Boston."

"You've found someone else." Mom caught my gaze and held it, confirming the significance with a swift nod of her head.

"I think so, yes. Clementine's daughter, Marguerite." I wouldn't tell her what I suspected about Hugh. If Hugh M. Morales wasn't him, it would be too cruel to get her hopes up.

"She must be a hundred."

"In her nineties, certainly. Perhaps at the time of life when people think about passing material things along to their rightful owners."

"Maybe." Mom sounded doubtful. "Where will you stay?"

"I've booked a room in a big hotel right in her neighborhood."

"Sounds expensive."

"I still have a lot of hotel points left from my job." I did, though only enough for a couple of nights. I hated to use them for this, but what was the investment, relative to a necklace worth two million dollars?

"I wish I could come." Much as she longed to know her mother's family, there was no way my mother was going to leave Maine when my sister needed her. Despite the long tentacles of her ancestors, my mother's face was fixed firmly toward the future, not the past.

"Get your coat," I said. "We're going to First Busman's this minute to rent a safety deposit box for the necklace. Otherwise, I'm not leaving."

"Okay," Mom sighed. "You win."

After I picked up Chris's truck, I took a detour and drove out toward the end of Westclaw Point. The note with the Black Widow had said, "For Windsholme," and so much of the story of my mother's family seemed to come back to that place. I felt pulled to it as if by a magnet. There was no one with a boat in the water who could take me out to Morrow Island, and I didn't want to ride across the cold ocean anyway. Looking from land would have to do.

Westclaw Point Road was plowed all the way to the end, a new town policy, in effect the last few years as more of the old places had been winterized. But most of the driveways I passed were snow clogged, the windows in the houses blank, empty for the season.

I pulled gingerly to the side of the road when I reached my friend Quentin's modern stone edifice. A wall of glass and marble, it erupted out of the rocky shore. The neighbors called it an eyesore. I teasingly called it Quentin's Fortress of Solitude. He wasn't there. He was off at one of his homes in the Caribbean or Manhattan or the Côte d'Azur. I imagined the scene when we handed over the money and happily paid him back. I wasn't sure he'd take it. He was a lover of the architecture of Windsholme and a major proponent of repairing and restoring, rather than demolishing, the old house.

The snow in Quentin's driveway would probably leave me in wet jeans for the drive south, but, called by Windsholme, I waded my way to his back deck. Windsholme stood in the distance across the water, sited at the highest point on Morrow Island. From this vantage point, the fire damage wasn't visible, just the clear, straight lines of the house, the slant of its slate roof, the twin sentries of its chimneys. Windsholme was beautiful, and I understood why Quentin loved this view of it. But the house was empty and dark; no smoke curled from its chimneys. Was there any arithmetic that made it worthwhile to save it, a relic of a bygone past? Was that what the person who sent the Black Widow to my mother meant for her to do?

Once the impulse to see the house was satisfied, I began to feel a little ridiculous for getting myself cold and wet and delaying my trip. I climbed down the stairs of the deck and returned to the truck.

Before I could climb inside, my childhood friend Jamie Dawes pulled his Busman's Harbor PD patrol car up behind the pickup. He emerged from the driver's side door. "Hey. Julia. What're you doing out here?"

"Checking on Windsholme."

"Still there?" He flashed his charming, surfer-dude grin.

"Yup. You?"

"Routine patrol."

I looked around the empty landscape. "There's no one out here."

"That's why it needs patrolling."

"I'm headed to Boston for a couple of days. Keep an eye on the family for me?"

"Of course. When's Livvie due?"

"Any day. We've already had one false alarm."

"Tough time for you to leave. What takes you out of town?"

I was acutely aware of the cold seeping through the wet legs of my jeans. This wasn't the time or place for a long explanation. "I'm going to meet Chris," I said, a partial truth.

"Oh." As I'd expected, it wasn't a topic Jamie wanted to explore further. "I'll look out for your family," he responded, turning back to his cruiser. "Take care of yourself in the big city."

"Will do," I called after him. He pulled away and I got in the truck, turned up the heater full blast, and headed toward Route 1. It would be dark before I got to Boston.

Chapter 13

Four hours later, I rattled through the dark streets of Back Bay in Chris's truck. I wondered why the heck I'd brought a vehicle to this city, a known circle of hell for driving in the best of times, made worse by a foot of dirty, slushy snow piled by the side of the roads. I'd sped out of Maine and across the New Hampshire border, and then I'd been caught in the most hellacious traffic jam I'd ever seen. "I'm going into the city, not out of it!" I yelled at the universe. Rush hour traffic should be going the other way. "Why is it like this? Where are all you people going?"

I found Marguerite and Hugh's town house, or at least I thought I did. As I cruised by slowly, lights streamed from every window. I passed one empty parking spot, but concluded I could never fit the truck into it. There was nothing to be done but to park at my hotel and then walk back.

Once the truck was in the hotel garage, I

figured I might as well check in. I took my suitcase to my room, a perfectly utilitarian shoe box. I was rapidly winding down, losing my nerve. What was I thinking, ringing the doorbell of total strangers at eight o'clock at night?

I stood at the window, looking over the city. I didn't know Boston well. I'd gone to prep school in New Hampshire and college in western Massachusetts, but trips to Boston had been rare and I'd never been on my own. From twenty-two stories up, the dirty snow was white and beautiful. The lighted windows of Back Bay, the black ribbon of the Charles River beyond it, and the streetlights and signs of Cambridge on the other side were warm and welcoming, a city at a human scale.

It was the lights that got me going again. The lights in the windows at Marguerite's house. She was home. Maybe Hugh Morales was there with her. This was the time to go. No reason, and even possible some risk, to putting it off. I hadn't taken my coat off. I pulled my gloves back on and headed outside.

Once I was walking, I was happier. Like my dear Manhattan, Boston was a city meant to be experienced on foot. The restaurants along Newbury Street were filled with diners, and even when I turned off onto Dartmouth Street, there were people everywhere, rushing home from work or to an evening activity. The practical Bostonians wore boots that gripped the sidewalk and long coats that hid their clothes.

As I approached Marguerite's brownstone,

my heart thumped and I slowed my pace. What was I doing? But the light over the front door beckoned me, welcomed me. I walked up the stone steps and pushed the bell before my courage gave out.

There was a rustling sound inside and the door flew open. I immediately recognized the woman who stood in the front hall. Her thick, wavy hair and deep-set brown eyes were unmistakable.

"Rose? Rose Morrow?" I said. "I thought you lived in San Francisco."

"Julia Snowden!" she cried. "What a shock. Come in, come in. We're all here."

Rose led me down a grand hallway clad almost to its high ceiling in warm oak wainscoting. How did she know who I was? Who was the "we" that was "all" here? My mind spun, grasping for the edges of some possible explanation.

We passed through a double doorway into a formal front room filled with antiques. A small group was gathered there and, if the scattering of china cups was any indication, they were having after-dinner coffee.

"Julia," Rose said. "May I present our cousin Marguerite Morales. Marguerite, this is Julia Snowden, Jacqueline's daughter."

The woman seated in the straight-backed chair was ancient and tiny, her white hair parted in the center and woven into two braids that were pinned to her head. She put one of her hands out to me. "Ellen's Jacqueline?" she said, dark eyes dancing. "Julia, I'm so glad you've come. How did you hear, dear?"

Before I could ask, "Hear what?" Rose hustled me off to meet the rest of the people in the room. "This is Marguerite's granddaughter, Tallulah," Rose said, presenting a woman in her early twenties with soft, round curves. "And Tallulah's husband, Jake."

I put my hand out to both of them, repeating their names in my head. Jake had a boyishly round face and kind brown eyes. Handshakes completed, Rose moved me across the room to where a man and a woman sat on a sofa. The woman appeared to be in her late fifties or early sixties. Her helmet of hair was an improbable shade of blond that went poorly with her olive complexion.

"This is Vivian, Tallulah's mother, Marguerite's daughter." Rose cleared her throat. "And this is her . . . fiancé, Clive." Clive was impeccably dressed, in a blazer and expensive shirt. He had a full head of caramel-colored hair and a trim physique, but then that wouldn't be unexpected in someone thirty years Vivian's junior. When Rose said the word "fiancé," Tallulah rolled her eyes at her husband, Jake.

"And finally . . ." Rose brought me to the back of the room where a large man stood against the wall. While the others were smartly but casually dressed, this man wore scrubs and his slightly bulging eyes were rimmed in red. "This is Paolo Paolini."

Paolo's red eyes filled me with dread about what I had to ask next. "Is Hugh home?" I asked. "Hugh Morales?"

There was a moment of stunned silence.

"We thought that was why you were here," Vivian said from across the room. "For the funeral. Hugh died Friday morning." *The day we'd received the package.*

Tears stung my eyes and the room spun a little. Rose Morrow put a reassuring hand on my arm and guided me to an overstuffed chair. "Hugh's dead?" I didn't know why I took it so hard. I'd never met the man, and if he was who I thought he was, until this morning I'd believed he'd been dead for more than thirty-five years. But even as I rationalized, I knew why I was so stunned. Because I had pictured myself as the heroine, triumphantly returning her beloved cousin to my mother. I'd been dying to see her face when I told her. My hopes burst like a balloon pricked by a pin. Thank goodness I hadn't mentioned my suspicions to Mom.

"He was ill," Rose said gently. "It was a blessing in the end."

"He knew it was coming," Vivian added. "He made all the arrangements, wrote his own obituary. We were talking final details when you arrived."

Paolo, still standing, took a tissue from the pocket of his scrubs and blew his nose.

They looked at me expectantly. *Questions. So many questions. Where even to start?*

"If you didn't know about Hugh, why are you here?" Vivian inquired.

I didn't know what to say. I was certain one of the people in that room knew why I was there. One of them had sent the Black Widow to my mother.

"It's a time for family," Marguerite said, as if it were as simple as that. "Rose, bring our new guest some coffee."

"Certainly." Rose moved to a cart that held a silver coffee service. She put a hand on the pot. "This is cold. I'll go along to the kitchen and get some from the machine. Anyone besides Julia?" When no one answered, she headed out the double doors into the long hallway.

"I'll come with you," I said, and scurried after her.

The town house's kitchen was in the basement. It was spare and not updated, a place for servants and not family, though I saw no sign of hired help. Rose took a china cup from an old-fashioned glass-fronted cabinet and poured coffee from a modern machine on the wooden countertop.

"How do you know who I am?" I demanded. "How long have you known about me?"

She raised an eyebrow, amused, not defensive. "I could ask you the same thing. But in answer to your question, I've known about you for years. You and your mother and your sister."

I was dumbfounded. "But how? There was never any communication."

"Sadly, that's true. My grandparents wrote to

your grandfather a few times, hoping to be a part of your mother's life, but he never responded, and as far as I know, all communication was cut off."

That had to be right after Hugh's disappearance, when Mom was still young enough my grandfather could stand as a gatekeeper. "How did you know what I look like?"

"I expect the same way you knew what I look like," Rose answered. "The Internet. You led a busy professional life in Manhattan, plenty of references to you on the web, photos of you at the companies your firm invested in, and so on. And there's been some publicity around the family clambake lately, not all of it good."

I nodded, acknowledging that was true. The murder on Morrow Island in the spring, followed by the fire at the mansion, had made the local papers. The Maine statewide papers too. "But how come no one seemed surprised when I showed up?"

"I was," Rose said. "But I'm delighted you're here. We'd better rejoin the others."

Chapter 14

Back in the formal living room, no one had moved. Paolo still stood against the wall, a wounded giant. Vivian was on the couch, every faux-blond hair in place, her makeup perfect. Clive, the fiancé, sat at the other end of the couch, wearing the self-satisfied look of a pure-bred Siamese cat. Tallulah and her husband, Jake, were on the bench of the grand piano, he facing the instrument, she away from it into the room. Despite the February weather, she had on a sleeveless sundress, which showed off a large tattoo of a bird on a tree branch that snaked over her left shoulder to her breast. Her eyes were surrounded with heavy black makeup. She put her chin in her hand and stared at me with her raccoon eyes. Whatever they'd been talking about, the conversation had stopped when Rose and I returned.

I sat in a straight-back chair not far from Marguerite. She, frail but powerful, broke the uncomfortable silence. "We've been laboring under a misunderstanding," she said. "We assumed you'd arrived because our attorney had been in contact with you. Or rather with your mother. She's been left a bequest."

Aha, here it comes. Hugh left Mom the Black Widow. "A bequest?"

"A small bequest of personal property. Don't get your hopes up," Vivian said. "Hugh's half ownership in this house goes to my mother, as it should, along with his financial portfolio. The family attorney will be here at ten o'clock to-morrow morning. He can explain it to you then. I suggest, if you are going to act for your mother, that you obtain her power of attorney while you are here. But then, it will be some time until the estate is distributed. Perhaps she will grace us with her presence as time goes on."

The long day hit me all at once. I felt as though my brain had turned to mush. "I have so many questions."

Marguerite felt for her cane and stood, stomping it on the wooden floor. "They will keep until the morning. I'm tired now. See you at ten."

The others stood as well, and it was clear Marguerite had the last word. Rose saw me to the door, giving me a quick hug before I set out. "I'm so happy to know you," she said.

"Me too," I answered. "Me too."

Unusually, the trip back to the hotel seemed far longer than the walk over. The temperature had dropped and the slush on the sidewalks had frozen, meaning I had to concentrate on every step. I stumbled into the hotel lobby and took the elevator straight to my floor.

I intended to call Mom, but as I pulled off my boots, a glance at my phone told me it was after ten o'clock. She was undoubtedly asleep. I'd call in the morning. I hadn't decided how much to tell her and how much to save until I got home.

I'd just drifted off when my phone erupted, startling me awake. I looked at the display. 11:06 PM. *Mom!* I answered, heart pounding. What was she doing up?

"Julia, I'm calling because Page and I are on our way up the peninsula to stay at Livvie's house."

"Is Livvie—"

"She's fine, but she's had another false alarm. I want to be available if I'm needed. There's another storm coming through over the weekend and I would hate to be stuck in the harbor if Livvie goes into labor. Fee and Vee will take care of Le Roi."

Mom's words were reassuring, but her voice quivered a touch. My chest squeezed. "Are you sure Livvie's all right?"

"She's fine." Mom said it more forcefully this time, with a touch of impatience. "What's happening there? Did you find out who sent the necklace?"

"Maybe. I met your cousin Marguerite." I waited for a reaction, but none came. I heard the engine of her ancient Mercedes rev. I wouldn't tell her about Hugh yet. Not while she was driving late at night, already concerned about Livvie. Besides, no one at the house on Marlborough Street had exactly confirmed Hugh Morales's identity. "Mom, I may need your power of attorney to straighten everything out down here. I'll call Cuthie Cuthbertson in the morning."

"Does that mean the Black Widow could be ours?"

"Not clear. Not clear at all. Don't get your hopes up."

"All right. I can stop by Cuthie's in the morning if needs be. I've arranged my shifts so I can be home when Page gets out of school."

"We'll talk in the morning."

Chapter 15

I spent some time in the hotel business center the next morning going back and forth with Mom and Cuthie to get the power of attorney. Mom had stopped in his office on her way to work and was frazzled and in no frame of mind to ask many questions.

After Mom did the paperwork and rushed out, Cuthie kept me on the phone. "What's going on, exactly, Julia? I assume this is in regard to the tiara we discussed."

"It's not a tiara, it's a necklace, and yes, this is related. Or at least I think it is." I filled him in on my tale of long-lost relatives and the long-lost Black Widow.

"And you're convinced this Hugh Morales is your mother's cousin, the late Hugh Morrow?"

"I am, but I've no more proof than I had yesterday morning when I found Hugh Morales on the web. The family attorney is showing up

at the town house at ten. I assume I'll know
more then." I had a sudden thought. "Do you
think I need my own attorney at this meeting?"

Cuthie's trademark baritone traveled across
the airwaves in his most soothing tones. "What
did they say Jacqueline was left?"

"A small, personal bequest."

"Let's not prepare for battle yet. Find out
exactly what his will says. And see if there's an
inventory with it that includes the necklace. If
this Hugh owned it, he must have had it insured.
Call me after the meeting. If you do need your
own attorney, I have some friends down there I
can recommend."

"Thank you, Cuthie. Thanks for everything."

Jake, Tallulah's young husband, answered the
door at Marlborough Street. "It's you," he said.
"Come in." He helped me out of my coat and
hung it on a tree in the hall. He seemed like a
nice enough guy, with an earnest manner that
went with the boyish face.

I left my boots in the tray by the front door
and slipped into a pair of flats. I'd dressed in a
black pencil skirt, crisp white blouse, and black
tights. I looked like a waitress, but it was the best
of what I'd brought with me. "Is Rose around?"

"Kitchen," Jake answered, inclining his head
toward the floorboards.

"Thanks."

Downstairs, Rose was bent over the sink, fin-
ishing up the breakfast dishes.

"Morning."

She nodded in acknowledgment. I grabbed a towel and started on the items in the dish rack. I didn't see a dishwasher in the outdated kitchen.

"How did you sleep?" Rose asked.

"Just okay."

"I can imagine. This must all be very strange for you." She rinsed off a frying pan and put it in the rack. "You can ask me questions, if you want. And I know you do."

"Is Hugh Morales really Hugh Morrow, your uncle?"

Rose turned to look at me. "Yes."

"How long have you known?"

"Since I was twenty-five, right after my grand-mother died."

"Did your grandparents know Hugh was alive?"

"Absolutely not. That's why I inherited every-thing." She put another dish in the rack. "I was only a year old when my dad died. My mother had given up her career to stay home with me. Dad had no life insurance. He was so young. So we lived with my grandparents until my mom got a job and got back on her feet. We moved out when I was three, but stayed nearby. They never warmed to my mother."

Rose paused, reacting to my expression. "Some of it was race. Some of it was class. They could never quite grasp that though Mom's father was a plumber, she'd graduated in the same Stanford Law class as their son. When my par-ents married, there was a complete break with dad's parents. My father worked at the law firm with his father every day, but according to my mother, the two couples never spent any family time together and my grandparents never even met me until after Dad died. At that point, they reached out to us. Once she got a job, my mom worked long hours and they filled in the gaps. To me, they were nothing but loving grand-parents.

"I was nineteen when Mom died. Aneurysm. Dad's parents became even more important then. Their house was the place I went on school breaks, where I spent my summers. They stepped in for my mother."

Rose had spent her college vacations at the home where Hugh had refused to go for his. "My mother had the impression Hugh's parents were difficult," I said. An understatement.

"I have that perspective from my mother," Rose agreed. "I'd love to believe I turned them around with my sheer adorableness, but I think what really happened is they mellowed. Losing two sons knocked the edges off them. I was their last chance, all they had left. They weren't drinking by the time I remember them, either, which Mom said was a huge part of the problem."

"I can't figure out why Hugh never mentioned you to my mom."

Her brow creased. "He didn't? He was in prep school by the time I moved into his parents' house, and he hardly ever came back to San Francisco. Maybe a toddler wasn't important to a teenaged boy." Her voice sounded regretful, or resentful, but she continued her story. "My grandfather died during my first year in medical school, my grandmother in my third year." She paused. "They left their entire estate to me. On the one hand, I never had to worry about medical school debt. On the other, it was a lot of responsibility for someone no older than Tallulah, and a lot of loss to absorb in a compressed amount of time. I arranged my grandmother's funeral and not long after set about cleaning out the house. I was going to have to sell it. Normal people can't live in a place that big. The task was enormous. There was four generations of stuff, some of it quite valuable, and some of it total junk. I was fitting the work in between my studies and trying to spend a little time with my husband-to-be. It was going to take years to do the job.

"One day as I worked a man showed up on the front stoop. He said his name was Hugh Morales and he had known my grandparents. He wondered if I needed help." She put the final dish, a ceramic creamer, into the dish rack and took off the flowered apron she wore. "I recognized who he really was right away. This was more than twenty years ago. He still looked similar enough to all the photos of him around the house. But I didn't say anything. I was afraid it would scare him off and I really, really needed the help. I had to get back to my studies. In the end, he arranged everything. Had all the pieces appraised. Auctioned the valuables off, gave the rest away. The house was gleaming when I turned it over to the realtor. Hugh never asked for payment, except for a few small items I knew had been his. My grandparents had never changed a thing in his room. Or my father's. That's what comes of having too much money and space."

"When did Hugh tell you who he really was?"

"At some point, he figured out I knew, but he never said anything and neither did I. He never said the words to me until a few days ago." As she talked she put away the dishes I'd dried with the easy knowledge of someone in a familiar kitchen. "He came to San Francisco every other year to visit with me and my family. He was a particular favorite of my son's. And I would visit him whenever I came to Boston for a medical conference. Eventually, he introduced me to Marguerite and I got to know the others, Vivian and Tallulah."

"How did Hugh find them? The connection was generations back."

"As I understand it, Marguerite found him. She remembered her two much older half brothers, even though there'd been no contact in years. As a little girl, she'd been at Windsholme with them. She tracked down my grandparents and contacted my dad when he was at Harvard. This house became his home away from home here in Boston. He stayed with her whenever he didn't go to San Francisco for school breaks, and through him Marguerite met Hugh."

A wave of emotion broke over me and threatened to pull me under. I was delighted to have found my mother's relatives, but she would be devastated to learn about all this family life that had been going on without her. These people knew where she was all this time. Why had no one reached out?

"Tell me about the others," I asked, pushing down the feelings.

"Marguerite is amazing. She fought in Spain against Franco and married a Spaniard."

I nodded. That part I knew from Floradale Thayer back at the Busman's Harbor Historical Society.

"She's a little frail now at ninety-six, as you'd expect, but sharp as a tack. She still attends the ballet and the theater, even if she's no longer on the board of every arts organization in the city. She reads every day. Knowing her has enriched my life so much. She's taught me by example how to be old."

I felt a pang, thinking how much my mother's life would have been enriched if she too had a chance to know Marguerite.

"Tallulah's a good kid, as far as I can see. She and Jake are students at Berklee College of Music, here in Boston. They have a cabaret act. She sings, he accompanies her on the piano. They've played in clubs locally and are supposed to do a small tour this summer."

Musicians. "Was anyone else in the family musical?"

"The only one I know of was Hugh. He used to play that grand piano in the living room and the sound would fill the house. I loved listening to him."

"And Vivian?"

"Vivian is Vivian. I'm not sure how Marguerite ended up with a daughter like her. The kindest thing I can say is that Vivian has all of the romanticism that drove Marguerite to Spain, and none of the practicality that got her back alive."

"Clive isn't Tallulah's father." I stated it as a fact.

"Not hardly. Tallulah's father was husband number three. Clive's auditioning for the role of number six. Or seven. Like I said, Vivian's a romantic. She loves falling in love, but she doesn't have much staying power afterward. Clive is a 'tech executive.'" Rose didn't have to do the gesture for me to pick up on the air quotes.

"I used to be in the venture capital business, investing mostly in technology," I said.

"I know. I found you on the web, remember? But I wouldn't spread that information around or you'll have to listen to his awful investor presentation."

"You don't like him."

"No one here does. Besides Vivian, of course. She's besotted."

"Tell me about Paolo."

"He's a hospice nurse. Marguerite hired him so Hugh could die at home. He's been here a little more than two months. I met him when I came out in January, after the holidays. I don't know how Marguerite found him, but he's a caring and compassionate man, and an able nurse. A godsend."

"He seems really broken up about Hugh.

You'd think someone who does hospice work would be more detached."

"Medical people feel all the feelings," Rose responded. "Sometimes it's better to process them."

I hesitated. "Rose, what did Hugh die from?"

"Prostate cancer, very aggressive and very advanced by the time it was diagnosed."

We had sat down at the rough kitchen table after we'd finished the dishes. Rose gazed out the kitchen door and down the hallway.

"What happened a few days ago, when Hugh told you who he was?" I asked.

"He said, 'Rose, I am your uncle,'" she answered, using Darth Vader's voice.

I laughed and said, "No, really."

"He was sick and weak, but certain of what he wanted to say. 'As you've always suspected, I am your uncle, Hugh Morrow. I'm saying that name now, a name I haven't used in decades, because I need to tell you, I've left you nothing except a token amount in my will. I don't want any misunderstandings later.' I said, 'Hugh, how could you think I would ever object? I've been well provided for by my grandparents. In fact, in addition to my father's half, I got the part of the estate that should have been yours. I'm just grateful that I've known you and you've been in my life and brought Marguerite and her family into it too. Otherwise, I would have been alone.' And he said, 'I knew you'd understand.'"

I thought again of my mother, who wasn't well provided for, and who *was* left all alone.

"Rose, did you send my mother a package last week? Either at Hugh's request or on your own initiative?"

"A what?" Rose looked as blank as blank could be. Unless I very much misjudged her, she had no idea what I was asking her about.

The clatter of footsteps came down the stairs. Jake stuck his head through the kitchen door. "Lawyer's here. He's got some other guy with him."

"Coming." Rose stood. "Let's get this done."

Chapter 16

Rose, Jake, and I were the last ones into the living room. Everyone was in his or her place from the night before. Even Paolo Paolini stood against the back living room wall, though he wasn't in scrubs. Instead he wore khakis and a long-sleeved plaid shirt, both crisply ironed. I sat in my chair from the night before too, like it had already become my accustomed place.

Two men stood at the front of the room. The middle-aged one with the salt-and-pepper hair, wearing gold wire-rimmed glasses and an expensive-looking gray suit, was clearly the lawyer. The man beside him stared at each of us, as if memorizing our faces. His sport coat was shiny and the bottom of his pants had stains from the salt on the sidewalks. I wondered for a second if he might be a paralegal, but he emanated authority as he stood, stance wide, shoulders slightly back.

Uh oh. I'd seen that look before. He was a cop,

I was certain. I tensed, waiting for him to say something about a missing two-million-dollar necklace.

The lawyer took a seat in the dining chair that had been positioned next to Marguerite's. He cleared his throat. "I'm Adam Dickison, attorney for the deceased, Hugh Morales. I believe I know all of you, except . . ." He hesitated, looking at me.

"Pardon our manners, Adam," Marguerite said. "This is our cousin, Julia Snowden, Jacqueline's daughter."

"Jacqueline Snowden," Mr. Dickison repeated. "The bequest of personal items." The other man's head snapped around to stare at me.

Mr. Dickison cleared his throat a second time. He seemed reluctant to say whatever it was he needed to say. Finally, he began. "I know you had planned to have a memorial reception tomorrow in a private room at the Harvard Club, followed the next day by cremation and interment of the ashes, as per Mr. Morales's final instructions." He paused. "I'm afraid the latter will not be possible."

"Why not?" Vivian's cheeks glowed pink through layers of foundation and powder. "It's already been announced. The arrangements were in the obituary in the *Globe* this morning."

The lawyer turned to the man in the shiny coat. "Detective."

The man nodded and spoke. "Detective Salinsky, Boston police, Homicide. You will not be able to inter Mr. Morales the day after tomorrow because his remains have been removed from the funeral home to the state medical examiner's office."

No one said a word until, finally, Marguerite spoke. "Detective, what does this mean? My son was terminally ill." *Son? Hugh wasn't Marguerite's son.* Marguerite continued. "He died a long, lingering, horrible death, as every person in this room will tell you. I was grateful he could be home to be with us until the end. There is nothing for your medical examiner to investigate."

Salinsky's eyes softened. Who wouldn't feel for a woman in her nineties who had lost her son? "I am sorry, Mrs. Morales, but the department received information from a confidential source that Mr. Morales's death, though expected, was not a result of his illness, as you might have supposed. He was murdered."

Whoa. That wasn't the news I'd expected the cop to deliver. I felt like my body had taken a swift elevator ride and left my stomach at the top of the shaft.

In the back of the room, Paolo, who never seemed far from tears, pressed an eye with his wrist.

On the piano bench, Tallulah began to sniffle, and said, "I don't understand."

"I don't understand, either." Vivian's voice was harsh with vexation. "What confidential source?"

"If I told you," Salinsky replied in a more reasonable tone than the question deserved, "it wouldn't be confidential."

"Perhaps you'd best tell us," Marguerite said, "what the medical examiner found that has brought you here."

"I'm not able to disclose that yet. Officially, I don't have final results. I'm here because the department didn't want you to hear from the funeral home that the body had been removed, and to let you know cremation will not go on as scheduled. That is all I can say at this moment."

Attorney Dickison rose, his mouth turned down in discomfort. "I think, in the circumstances, we shouldn't go on with our discussion of the details of Mr. Morales's final wishes and the disbursement of his estate. You all know, except perhaps you, Ms. Snowden, the provisions of Mr. Morales's final will. He and Marguerite owned the town house as joint tenants, so that passes directly to her. She also gets his savings, stocks, and bonds. He expressed a wish that these assets be used for the upkeep and running of the house so that Marguerite could remain here as long as she wishes." He turned again to me. "Aside from small bequests of money to Vivian, Tallulah and Rose, he left his personal property, his books, and everything else to Jacqueline Snowden."

Dickison picked up his fat leather briefcase in one fluid motion. "I'll let you digest this news and discuss how you want to proceed with the memorial reception." He walked slowly toward the archway into the front hall, then turned. "If there is anything I can do, anything at all, you know where to reach me."

Detective Salinsky pulled out a handful of business cards and left them on the table next to Marguerite's chair. "These cards have my direct line. Call me if you have any questions or concerns."

"Concerns?" Vivian tossed her blond hair. "Concerns? I am way past concerns. I am furious."

"I'm sorry for your trouble, ma'am," Salinsky murmured.

"Not nearly as sorry as you are going to be."

Rose showed the two men out. The moment the door shut, there was a babble of voices, everyone talking over everyone else.

"Quiet!" Marguerite commanded. "They can hear you from the street."

"Who called the police?" Vivian demanded. "Which one of you brought them into this?"

"It might not have been one of us," Clive protested. "It could have been a colleague from work or one of his friends." It surprised me that of all of them, he was the one who took on Vivian.

"Don't be ridiculous!" Vivian snapped. "They said their good-byes weeks ago. There have been no visitors in this house, except her." She pointed at Rose.

Did all the others live here? I hadn't quite understood that.

"Rose is not a visitor," Marguerite said firmly. "She is family."

"This is all your fault." Vivian turned on Paolo. "If you had been with him at the end, as you should have been, his death wouldn't have been 'unattended' and we wouldn't be in this situation now."

"I told you," Paolo started, in a rolling Italian accent, "I stepped out for just a little while, thirty minutes only, to eat a late snack, and he went while I was gone. This is not uncommon with dying people. When they love you, they take the energy from you, they want to stay alive to please you. You had all come in to say good-bye that day. Rose was here at last. I believe he waited for her. He was done with what he had to do in this life, and when I left him, he let go and slipped into the next one. He was a very sick man."

"Exactly." Rose stood up. "Let's hope the medical examiner turns up nothing."

"If that's your hope, why did you call the police?" Vivian asked.

"I didn't," Rose protested.

Tallulah jumped to her feet from the piano bench. "Mummy, you are awful!" She burst into noisy sobs and rushed from the room. Jake ran out after her.

Marguerite sighed. "Let's be practical for the moment. Hugh's obituary ran in the paper this morning. Shall we go ahead with his memorial reception at the Harvard Club tomorrow and let the chips fall as they may on the interment? If we want to change things, we have very little time to get a notice to the *Globe*."

"I say, keep the reception," Rose said. "It's only the cremation and burial that's affected."

"Vivian?" Marguerite asked.

"Yes, yes. No point in calling any more attention to this mess than necessary. Maybe it will all blow over."

From the back of the room, Paolo nodded his agreement, not that anyone had asked him.

Marguerite turned toward me. "Julia, you'll stay for the reception?"

"Of course, she'll stay," Vivian said. "She wants to see what Hugh left her mother."

Marguerite glared at her daughter. "Vivian, that's beneath you."

I didn't think it was.

Vivian glanced at her watch. "Sorry," she mumbled, like a scolded child. "I have to go." She left the room, Clive following wordlessly.

"I'll go to the deli and get some sandwiches to share," Rose said. "We need milk and cream as well."

"Thank you, dear, for your thoughtfulness at this difficult time," Marguerite said. Salinsky's revelations seemed to have knocked the stuffing out of her. She looked every bit of her ninety-six years, and exhausted.

"I'll go too." I wanted to be helpful. I also wanted to get out of the house. How was I going to tell my mother that cousin Hugh had been alive, but now was not only dead, but he'd been murdered? The dread of that conversation emptied my brain of every thought, my body of every feeling.

"Rose can handle it, Julia," Marguerite said. "I think it's time you and I had a talk."

Chapter 17

When Rose left I moved to the chair next to Marguerite, where the lawyer had been. I inched it even closer and leaned in her direction.

"I imagine you have some questions for me." Marguerite grasped my forearm. I was surprised by her strength. She looked frail, but the hand on my arm channeled inner toughness. I had so many questions, I didn't know where to begin.

Marguerite took the reins of the conversation, thank goodness. "You were surprised to hear me refer to Hugh as my son."

Okay. Let's start there.

"I adopted him as an adult twenty years ago. I was at a crossroads financially. This house was in dire need of repairs and updating. I was going to have to sell it, or condo it and live in one small section. I think you'll agree, architecturally it's of a piece." She gestured toward the magnificent staircase. "I didn't want it chopped to bits. My father bought this house in 1888.

He brought my mother here after their wedding in 1919. My family is meant to be here. Hugh was a great lover of architecture, and family too, and he agreed. He invested his savings in the house. I already thought of him as my son. It seemed like the right time to make it official."

For such a great lover of family, Hugh had been outrageously cruel to my mother, and to his parents. That seemed to be his way. He turned up when he was needed—when my mother was lonely at boarding school, when Rose was overwhelmed by her grandparents' estate, when Marguerite needed money for her house—and then he left in the most dramatic fashion imaginable. Twice.

I wondered how Vivian, Marguerite's only child, felt about Hugh's adoption. I'd been worried Page, an only child for a decade, would resent a new sibling. What about four decades?

"But how did Hugh come to be here in the first place?" I asked. "How did Hugh Morrow become Hugh Morales, if you adopted him years after his disappearance and 'death'? How could he have done this to my mother?" It burst out of me. He'd put her through the agony of his disappearance, and then let her live with the sadness, guilt, and emptiness all those years. How could he have been only a three-hour drive away, alive and, until recent years, healthy?

Marguerite gave me a look, emanating from her hooded brown eyes. "He didn't mean to disappear. At least not at first. He told me he had a fight with a girl he liked and all he could think was to leave the party. That's the trouble with islands. You cannot get away from people you do not wish to see. So he hid aboard the boat your grandfather hired to take the party guests back to the harbor. When it docked he waited until all the guests had left, then walked away. He hitchhiked back to Cambridge with a tourist who was driving south toward his home in North Carolina. I'm sure the man never saw the news reports about Hugh's disappearance. He never came forward."

I should have realized, spending his summers on Morrow Island, Hugh would have his own friends, including girls. Mom had never mentioned a fight with a girl on the night Hugh disappeared. But then, she might have seen it as a motive for a young man to fling himself into a cold, dark sea. She had never said it, exactly in those words, but I knew that's what she feared most. That her cousin had killed himself.

"Hugh went to a college friend's apartment," Marguerite continued. "He was feeling low about the girl, and didn't look at the news or newspapers. I'm sure he knew your mother and grandfather would miss him, but he had no idea about the search. It wasn't like it is today. There wasn't endless press coverage about a twenty-one-year-old man who left a party."

She sensed my skepticism. "He was a foolish young man," she said. "When he did realize, he was horribly embarrassed about all the fuss, but the more he thought about it, the more he saw it as a solution to a problem."

"What problem was that?"

Marguerite looked down at her hands in her lap. They had dark age spots, and long, graceful fingers like my mom's. They were the first bit of family resemblance I'd spotted.

"It must have occurred to you that for a young man to spend not just his summers, but so many of his school holidays with distant cousins, something must be terribly wrong at home. Arthur and Hugh's father was a tyrant. He was one of the top lawyers in the city and he demanded his boys follow in his footsteps. He browbeat Arthur into attending Stanford Law and joining his firm. Arthur was in his first year working there when he went overboard into San Francisco Bay. There were many who believed it was not an accident."

So Rose lived in the shadow of a suicide, as my mother did.

"Hugh's father was a bully who used his voice, his fists, and his money in his attempt to completely control the lives of his sons. The boy's mother was a person who cared only about reputation and image. The only opinions that mattered were those of the people outside her home. Their father could yell, bully, and even beat the boys as long as the neighbors and her friends didn't find out. Hugh dreaded graduating from college. He'd shared this with me and I'd told him to run off, go to Europe as I had as a young woman. Live abroad. Start over. But Hugh didn't believe he could ever escape the long arm of his father. When he was missing, and then presumed dead, he saw his chance. He did start over. By never volunteering he was alive."

"And you supported this?" Hugh had been twenty-one, but Marguerite was fifty-eight, if I calculated right, with a grown child of her own when Hugh disappeared. Surely, she must have had some empathy for Hugh's parents.

Marguerite shook her head, the braids that wound around it moving slightly. "I didn't know about the deception at first. I'm telling you now what he told me later, when he returned here. After a couple of weeks in Cambridge, he did take off, traveling constantly. He learned the tricks of building a new identity from his fellow travelers on the road. He turned up here the first time two years after his disappearance. I begged him to call his parents, but he refused. He said if I told them, he'd disappear from my life as well. He only stayed two weeks that first time. I think it was a test, to see if he could trust me, though he didn't return again until after his parents had him declared dead."

"Why do you think he came back?"

"Because, like me, Hugh had a strong feeling for family. His parents may have been awful in their different ways, but Hugh longed for an affiliation. I'm sure that's why he returned to me, and why he sought out Rose after his parents passed away. He didn't want his parents' money. To him it was a part of the leash his father had used to control him. After so many years on the road, his needs were modest by then, anyway. But he wanted to know his niece.

"After his parents had him declared dead, he came to live with me. We called him Hugh Morales, even then, and I told my friends he was a nephew of my late husband's. He rebuilt his life and he was a part of rebuilding this neighborhood. He became a realtor, an expert in historic buildings. When my mother moved into this house in 1919, this neighborhood was the anchor of a genteel Boston. Then came the Depression, the war. My contemporaries fled to the suburbs, but I stayed. I stayed through the rooming houses, and the hippies, and then the yuppies, who bought the houses and converted them to condos. I stayed through it all. Hugh loved the house as much as I did. Aside from Morrow Island, I think it was the only place he thought of as home."

"Rose told me when you were on Morrow Island as a child, you stayed at Windsholme."

"Ah, what a house that was. So grand, so soaring, so sumptuous. But you know it."

"Not really. I've only seen it empty, dirty, and run down. I try to imagine what it was like in its day."

"The perfect place for a child. So many hiding places—in the great house, on the grounds. There was a rose garden right beside the house, surrounded by a tall hedge. And beyond that, a playhouse, a mini version of Windsholme." She had closed her eyes, as if carried back by the memories.

"The rose garden is gone, but the playhouse is still there. Now it's surrounded by woods."

"I am glad to hear that. Windsholme is a special property, you know. It was designed by Holden Hodgman, his only house in Maine, and the grounds were designed by a student of Frederick Law Olmsted."

"I know." My friend Quentin was always going on about the house and what an architectural gem it was. "Why did you stop going to Windsholme?"

"The house wasn't my mother's. She was given the right to use it for life, but my father left it to my half brothers, and then William bought out Charles's portion." I knew this from Floradale Thayer. "Even before the stock market crash in twenty-nine, William had lost most of his money. He was barely holding on to the property. And after the crash, it all became unsupportable. The house, the grounds, the servants. And the last night my mother and I spent there, something happened. A valuable necklace was stolen during a wild party."

"Was the necklace ever found?" I kept my voice as casual as I could.

"No one knew who took it, though there were many suspicions. Some said it was a maid, though I always thought that sounded made up, a story to move suspicion away from the family and their fancy guests. Some people thought your great-grandfather William stole it, to sell to keep his homes and his company. Some even thought my mother made up the story of the theft, so she could sell it. Those were desperate times. Only Hugh's branch of the family in San Francisco prospered, and that was later. The whole affair soured my mother on the family. She fell out with her stepsons and their children after that."

"But you found Arthur."

"When my mother died, I was alone. I knew I had half brothers who were much older. I found the family. When Arthur matriculated at Harvard, I contacted him."

"I am sorry about Hugh. It must be difficult for you." I meant what I said. In a short time, I'd come to like this elderly woman a great deal.

"It truly has been like losing a son." Her voice remained strong, but turned husky. "I am grateful that at the end, we were able to bring him home. He wanted to die here, and thanks to his generosity in helping me maintain this house and keep it in the family, I was able to give something back to him. I hired Paolo and that made it all possible. I'm an old woman. I have limited resources. But that I could do." She sighed. "But enough of that. I'd love to hear about your family, but this morning's unexpected news has worn me out. I must go rest. We'll talk again."

"You should meet my family. You should come to Morrow Island in the summer."

"At my age, I don't make plans six months in advance. And I'm not sure I'm up to the journey. But thank you. I should like to know your mother. With Hugh gone, there's no impediment left."

Marguerite used her cane to push herself to her feet. I jumped up to help her. "Thank you, dear. I shall go up to rest." We walked to the bottom of the stairway. She sat on a mechanical chairlift that would move her to the second floor. "You should go see Hugh's room," she said. "His books and whatnots. They're going to belong to your mother. Second floor, third door to the left."

The machine moved her slowly up the stairs. It was a graceful exit, almost like she was ascending to heaven.

Chapter 18

I waited until I heard Marguerite's door close at the top of the stairs, and then started up. Her room was at the back of the house. Down a long hallway were three doors off to the left, one to the right, and then another door at the other end that must have led to the room facing Marlborough Street. Every door was closed. The hallway was narrow and dark, much different from the generous proportions of the rooms downstairs. I moved to the third on the left and knocked lightly, not wanting to intrude if I had the wrong room. The door opened an inch and I pushed it wider.

There was no mistaking the look of the sick room. At the sight of the hospital bed, stripped bare, my heart squeezed and memories of my father's illness flooded back. Mom, Livvie, and Sonny had tended to him during the long months of his cancer, shuttling him to treatments, and finally sitting by his bedside in the days and nights before his death. I'd returned to Busman's Harbor for the occasional weekend or holiday, telling myself it was all I could do in the face of a busy career and my life in New York. My father understood and supported me, of that I was certain, but my absence, my inattention, was the greatest regret of my life.

There was other equipment scattered—a hospital table, a commode in the corner, and a metal pole used for bags of medication—but at its core, it was a masculine room, decorated in rich brown colors. I closed the door behind me for privacy. There was a double bookcase and a simple oak bureau on the opposite wall. The room had a single window, a result of the town house being on a corner.

I knelt by the bookcase to look at the titles. Of all Hugh's possessions, his books would tell me the most about him. I was grateful for some quiet time to absorb the world-shaking news of the last twenty-four hours.

Cousin Hugh liked history and biography, with a particular interest in the Civil War. There was a set of old notebooks he must have used to study for his real estate license back in the 1980s. I wondered why he hadn't discarded them. And then I found it—*A History of the Morrow Ice Company.* Cousin Hugh had a copy. I laughed out loud. No longer was I beholden to Floradale Thayer. Once the book passed to Mom, she could read it, and Livvie and Chris, and Page when she was a little older. I pulled the book from the shelf and cradled it in my arms.

The door opened and Paolo Paolini stepped in. "Who's here?" he asked, his voice more curious than accusatory.

"It's me, Julia. I'm on the floor behind the bed."

He moved farther into the room and closed the door behind him. "You like the books? Mr. Hugh, he loved books, so much. He read almost until the end, and in the last month, they read to him, the family. Mrs. Morales read to him, and Mrs. Vivian. He liked Mr. Jake to read to him the most. Very expressive, he said. He could listen to Jake for hours. Mrs. Tallulah read to him too, but he liked her to sing. Only Rose didn't read to him, because she arrived just before he died."

"Rose told me she got here in time to say good-bye."

Paolo nodded. "This is true. She got here late Wednesday night, spent Thursday with Mr. Morales, and he died in the early hours of Friday."

"I don't know how you do it," I said. "To know from the beginning that you will be there at the end."

He regarded me with his big, sad eyes. "When you are needed most, that is when the work is most rewarding."

It was a lovely sentiment and I admired him for it. I didn't think I could do it, especially again and again.

"Mr. Morales spoke often of your mother and grandfather and their many kindnesses," Paolo told me. "He believed he had done your mother a great wrong, though he never confessed to me what it was. It weighed on him more than anything else in his life."

I didn't know what to say to that. Every single person, including my mother, who had ever spoken to me about Hugh had talked of what a decent, kind man he was. But he had deceived and hurt my mother grievously, this woman about whom he spoke so fondly.

"Paolo, before he died, did Mr. Morales ask you to mail a small package?"

His face was as uncomprehending as Rose's had been. "No. I mailed nothing for him, not even a letter." Paolo moved to the doorway and put his hand on the knob, preparing to take his leave. "You should look in the top bureau drawer," he said. "That is where the things of value for your mother will be."

I thanked him and stood. He nodded and went out, closing the door behind him.

I looked back at the books. An old-fashioned scrapbook lay on its side on the bottom shelf. I pulled it toward me gently. My heart leapt with excitement. What would it be? Photos of Hugh and Arthur as boys? Or pictures of my mother and grandfather on Morrow Island? I opened the big front cover.

There was a newspaper clipping from the *Busman's Harbor Register*, announcing my parents' engagement. On the next page was the article about their wedding. "The bride wore an ivory gown that had been worn by her mother." There was the announcement of my birth, and two years later of Livvie's, along with lots of articles about the Snowden Family Clambake, from YOUNG COUPLE TRIES THEIR LUCK WITH AN OLD MAINE TRADITION, to stories about the clambake's booming success. "I could feed more tourists if I could find more people to hire," my father said one year.

The scrapbook was entirely about my family. It was overwhelming, both flattering and more than a little creepy. I didn't know what to think. *Why? Why would someone do this?*

There were stories about me in the elementary school play, and Livvie on the swim team, reports I'd made the honor role, and what Livvie had been up to with the Brownies. Then I disappeared to prep school, but Livvie was represented during the high school years, swimming to state records and championships, going to the junior prom. Then came her wedding picture, shot from the neck up to hide her pregnant belly, Sonny behind her looking uncomfortable in a jacket and tie. I kept turning pages. Notices that I'd made Dean's List at college. The announcement of Page's birth. My grandfather's obituary. My father's obituary. On the last page, articles about the murder on Morrow Island and photos of Windsholme, burned.

I sat cross-legged, not moving, barely breathing, the big book in my lap.

* * *

Minutes ticked by. The door opened and Tallulah came in. She walked toward the bed, then spotted me behind it on the floor. "You found the scrapbook." She sounded happy, not surprised to see me, and not at all worried about my reaction to finding my family's life documented by an allegedly dead relative.

"You know about this?" I was incredulous.

She sat down on the high hospital bed, swinging her legs and peering at me with her raccoon eyes. She wore a sleeveless yellow sundress, a stark contrast to the weather outside. I studied her tattoo. The flowering branches of a tree, a cherry I thought, ran from her back, over her left shoulder down to the top of her breast. Below her clavicle, a small bird perched, dull and gray, in contrast to the blossoms around it. I wondered about her psyche. What caused her to make this songbird, obviously a representation of herself, so plain in contrast to its opulent surroundings?

"I looked at Hugh's scrapbook all the time when I was little," she said. If she'd noticed me staring at the tattoo, she didn't acknowledge it. She must be used to people looking. "You and your sister were like girls in a fairy tale to me," she continued, "living on an island with a mansion and a playhouse, a beach and a magical woods."

"Hugh told you about us?" I was surprised. The scrapbook read like a secret obsession.

"I begged him for stories about you. He made

them up. You and your sister went on so many adventures. I longed for a sister to have adventures with."

There was a concept; you living your life with no idea you were a character in someone else's fairy tales. "Why didn't any of you contact us? We're real people."

"Hugh forbid it. He said it had to do with keeping the secret of who he really was, but as I got older, I thought he was embarrassed about deceiving your mom."

"Was everybody in on this?" I was incredulous.

"I always knew about you. I can't remember a time of not knowing. Mummy and Granny knew, of course, and Rose. We all looked at the scrapbook. Hugh never tried to hide it. In fact, the opposite. He'd look through it with us. But no one else knew. I was told never to say anything outside the house."

"Does Clive know about us?"

She shrugged. "Probably. Mummy will have told him. Or maybe even Hugh said something when Clive was in here reading to him. Hugh talked a lot about your mother at the end."

Paolo had said that too. Hugh had talked about Mom, but he hadn't called her. "Tallulah, did Hugh ask you to send a package to my mother?"

She didn't hesitate. "No. He never did." She stood and walked toward the door. "I'll leave you to go through his things."

I looked down again at the scrapbook, still open to the last page, the photo of the ruined mansion. The note with the Black Widow had said, "For Windsholme." It was clearer than ever Hugh meant us to use the necklace to restore the house. But why didn't he say so? And why the anonymous mailing if he meant my mother to have it? I felt sure the necklace would turn up in the inventory of "personal items" he'd left her, but who else in the house knew that?

Chapter 19

I stood up, stomping a foot that had fallen asleep. I was at a bit of a loss. I'd learned so much and advanced so little. Paolo had said everything of value was in the bureau. I limped over to take a look.

The oak bureau was a simple one, with two small drawers on top and larger ones below. I pulled out the top drawer on the left and found socks, neatly paired. The other top drawer held flotsam and jetsam, a jumble of crumpled receipts, cheap pens, pennies, and stamps. I riffled through the paper, hoping there was a note for my mother. If I couldn't bring her Hugh, maybe I could bring her his thoughts, his apologies for what he had done. But nothing like that appeared.

I found a leather case, about the size of a paperback book, in the back of the drawer. When I finally got the case to open, its lid snapped up with such force I jumped. The contents were unremarkable. A broken men's watch, some tie tacks. There was a pair of gold cuff links engraved with the initials AWM. I supposed they had been Arthur's. Maybe Rose had given them to Hugh when he cleaned out her grandparents' house. She said he'd taken nothing, but that didn't mean he hadn't accepted some tokens. I wondered if she would want the cuff links back. I had no doubt Mom would offer them to her. There was also a man's signet ring, not something I could picture anyone I knew wearing.

"What are you doing? Get out of there!"

I hadn't noticed the door open an inch or so. Vivian Morales Whatever-Whatever-Whatever pushed it farther and angled herself into the room. "You have no right to be in here. No right at all."

I looked around the spare room. If you removed the evidence of illness, it was the modest room of a modest man. Did she think there was something valuable here, a necklace, perhaps? "I'm sorry," I said. "Marguerite said I should look around in here at the—"

"The what? The treasures your ill-deserving mother stands to inherit? Did she look after Hugh all his life? Did she take him in when he was alone in the world with no identity, no place to live, and no way to make a living? No, she did not. My mother did all of that. She deserves his things. I can't think what was in his head when he left his personal property to your mother.

And, as for what my mother may or may not have said you could do, she is old. Ancient, in fact, and easily influenced and confused. You should be ashamed for taking advantage of her."

To me, Marguerite seemed to be the opposite of easily influenced or confused. And as for my mother, she would have loved to have done any of those things for Hugh, but he never gave her the opportunity. I looked around the room. I wasn't sure Mom would want any of Hugh's old junk after what he'd done to her. But that still left the problem of the necklace.

I snapped the lid of the leather case shut and put it back in the drawer. I didn't bother asking if she'd mailed a package for Hugh. I had no doubt that if the Black Widow had ever passed through Vivian's hands, it never would have arrived in Busman's Harbor. "Excuse me." I walked past Vivian into the hallway.

"I never." She stalked to the door at the opposite end of the hall from her mother's room, opened it without knocking, and slammed it behind her.

I had left the room as Vivian had ordered. A part of me wanted to linger, simply because she'd ordered me to go, but there wasn't much left to see. The door on the opposite side of the long hallway was open. I peeked in. It was a bathroom, the only one on the floor from the look of things. The old tub had been replaced with a walk-in shower, probably to accommodate Marguerite or Hugh's physical condition, but other than that, nothing had been updated in ages. Tiny black and white tiles covered the floor, and the pedestal sink was crowded with toothbrushes and toothpaste tubes along with a razor and shaving cream. It looked more like a bathroom college students shared than one for grown people. The mirrored door of the medicine chest hung open over the sink, a jumble of makeup and prescription medications inside.

I backed out of the room and nearly into Clive. "Excuse me. I'm sorry."

"No worries." We did a little dance in the tight hallway where he moved to his left and I moved to my right and then we did the opposite.

"I understand you're raising money for a technology company," I said. Rose had warned me to avoid the subject, but I couldn't resist. "What does your product do?" I was curious to see what kind of an entrepreneur he was. If he was a marketing person, he would offer to show me his "deck," the PowerPoint slides that contained his investor presentation. If he was a technology person, he'd want to show me a demo of the product.

"You wouldn't understand." Clive attempted to push past me.

That annoyed me, so I stood in his way. "Try me." Rose knew I'd worked in venture capital in Manhattan, but it seemed possible the others in the house knew me only through Hugh's scrapbook. My life after college was a blank for them.

He glanced around the confined space. "This is neither the time nor the place, but if you must know, my company's product, the GimmeThat! App is a point of purchase credit system. It's an Uber for Bitcoin for Millennials."

What a mouthful.

Clive relaxed into his pitch. "Say you're walking past a shoe store, and you see a pair of Jimmy Choos you really like. You scan the barcode with a little device attached to the phone, and bing, bang, boom, the GimmeThat! App purchases the shoes and has them sent to your house."

"So your invention is the app and the barcode scanner?"

"Much more than that. GimmeThat! is the entire ecosystem in which the product is purchased. We're revolutionizing retail, baby!" In his enthusiasm, he'd forgotten his objections to telling me.

"So you're partnering with the credit card companies?"

"No, we're competing with credit cards. Five years from now, there'll be no such thing. No need to partner or share the wealth with anyone."

I was confused. "But where does your company get the money to buy the shoes? Do your customers preload the card with money, like a phone card?" It would be a lucrative business model, but I couldn't see many users giving

GimmeThat! their money to hold for the next impulse purchase.

"That's the beauty of it. The retailer is so grateful for the business he gives us a percentage."

"But if he only gives you a percentage, how do you cover the full price of the shoes?" I tried to keep my voice light and curious, not challenging.

"With the percentage, as I explained. So many people will buy so much stuff, the money will roll in. That's what we'll use to pay off the retailers." He gave me a self-satisfied smile.

An Uber for Bitcoins for Millennials? More like a Pitch for a Ponzi Scheme for Patsies. There was no way anyone was falling for this. Clive was an idiot.

"I said you wouldn't get it." He must have sensed my skepticism, despite my best efforts. "Not much call for this sort of thing up in the great north woods where you live, but here in the city, believe me, millennials will eat up the GimmeThat! App."

I was sure they would, since as far as I could tell, they wouldn't be paying for those shoes. It wasn't that Clive didn't understand marketing or technology. The problem was more fundamental. He didn't understand basic concepts like *money* and *math*.

I had to get out of this. "Thanks for telling me about your idea."

"Not idea. GimmeThat! is a product and a company. Don't tell anyone else. I should have had you sign a confidentiality agreement."

I practically burst out laughing. "No worries. I won't tell a soul." I left him, feeling much better. I hadn't heard anything as funny as the GimmeThat! App pitch in days.

My phone vibrated in the pocket of my skirt. I pulled it out and glanced at the screen. Chris.

Chapter 20

I clambered down the stairs, stopped in the front hall to step into my boots and shrug on my coat, and went outside. I didn't want anyone to hear my conversation. The phone stopped vibrating. Chris had hung up.

He picked up on the first ring. "Hi, stranger. What you been up to?"

"How much time do you have?" I answered.

"That good, huh?"

"It's complicated. You?"

"It's not complicated at all. I'm standing in my bare feet on the deck of a gorgeous sailboat that's spit-shined within an inch of its life. It's eighty degrees out. How complicated can life be?"

I'd walked around the corner, my boots crunching with every step on a combination of melting ice and sidewalk sand. I laughed. "You're loving it."

"I am," he agreed. "This trip has really made me think."

"Think what?"

"Think, why am I spending my winters in frozen Maine?"

My stomach flipped. I sputtered into the phone. *Why was he spending . . . Because we ran a restaurant together, and practically lived together, that's why.* He was the reason I had given up my job, my apartment, and my life in New York to stay in Busman's Harbor, Maine. He had told me in no uncertain terms that he was dug in deep and wasn't moving.

Chris continued along, oblivious. "This is a good gig Joe has here. Maybe I'll bring the *Dark Lady* down next year." The *Dark Lady* was Chris's most prized possession, a wooden sailboat inherited from his uncle. Chris worked most of the year to support it, renting out his cabin in the summer season so he could live aboard her.

"The *Dark Lady* isn't big enough to take groups out for snorkeling or sunset cruises." My lack of enthusiasm was obvious in my voice, but Chris didn't pick up on it.

"Maybe private captaining, taking a couple or two out overnight or longer. Cuba's ninety miles from here. Pretty soon we'll be able to take people over for a night of music and dancing and bring them back the next day." Finally, he slowed down. "I'm fantasizing. This place will do that to you. But it's not like there's anything keeping me in Maine in the off season."

At last, he heard himself. There followed a rapid series of exhalations. "I mean, I mean . . ." But the damage was done. Weren't we building a business together in the off-season? And if that wasn't important, shouldn't it have been, "It's not like there's anything keeping *us* in Maine."

My phone buzzed again. A second call. Mom. It wasn't the time or place for this discussion anyway. "Chris, I have to take another call."

"Cool." He sounded like a prisoner given a reprieve by the executioner. "We're off to lunch. I was checking in to see how you were doing."

Better before this call.

I pressed the screen to end Chris's call and picked up Mom's. "Julia?"

"Hi, Mom. Why are you calling from work?" Mom had limited breaks during her shifts at Linens and Pantries and she didn't use them for social calls.

"I'm not at work. I'm at the hospital with Livvie."

"Is this it?" What would it mean if I left this whole mess in Boston and went home?

"Another false alarm from the look of things. Sonny took his dad to a lobstermen's meeting in Augusta. He wouldn't have gone except he knew I'd look after Livvie and Page. He'll be back before dinner. They're doing some tests on Livvie, a sonogram, and monitoring the baby's heart rate, but we'll probably go home."

"You sound worried."

"Livvie's exhausted. She's so big she can't sleep. I don't want her going into real labor already worn out. I'm sure it will be fine." My mother was the queen of the stiff upper lip.

"Do you want me to come home?"

"There's no need. Come home when you're done with the business there."

"I'll call later from the hotel and fill you in."

"Thanks."

It was only after we'd hung up that I realized my mother had no real reason to call me. She was worried, reaching out for a comforting voice.

I'd walked all the way around the block. As I approached Marguerite's house, Rose appeared from the other direction, carrying two cloth shopping bags packed to their tops. I hurried to her. "Let me take one of those."

She handed me a bag and we moved toward the house. "What are you doing out here— running away? I know it's been a lot," she said.

"I stepped out to take a phone call from my mom. My sister's very pregnant. Mom's worried."

Rose stopped on the sidewalk. "Olivia is having another child? That's wonderful."

"We call her Livvie. She's having a lot of false labor."

Rose nodded. "It's called prelabor now. It's not that it isn't doing anything, but it's not going to get a baby out."

We were at the town house's front walk. "This way." Rose led me under the stairs to a door. She turned a key in the lock and we were in the basement kitchen. From upstairs, I could hear someone, presumably Jake, playing a jazz riff on the grand piano.

Rose set me to work, putting sandwich halves on platters—rich, delicious looking and smelling deli sandwiches—and spooning salads into bowls. She emptied the contents of the second shopping bag—packages of wide, flat noodles, cans of tomato, cartons of creamy ricotta, and balls of mozzarella. "I'm making lasagna for dinner," she said. "Works for a crowd."

"You're like Cinderella, feeding the family, cleaning up."

"Hugh was the domestic one. He and Marguerite ran the house. After he got sick, and with Marguerite getting older, I'm not sure anyone has stepped up."

"They can't have been starving before you got here."

"There are a lot of take-out cartons in the re-cycle bin. Though that would be expected with a family member dying." She turned away, busy-ing herself assembling the sauce for the lasagna.

At last, we carried it all up to the dining room and put the food on the long table. Rose went to the front hall and called, "Lunch is here!"

Jake was the first to arrive, looking eager and hungry. He took a plate and loaded it up. Tallu-lah followed close behind. Paolo came in, took a sandwich, and sat at the table. I don't know why that surprised me. Probably because it was the first time I'd seen him seated when he was in the company of the family. Marguerite glided down the stairway on her moving chair, like Glinda the Good descending.

I hung back. I assumed everyone had a "regular" chair, and I didn't want to put any-body out. When they all began to eat and it was clear Vivian and Clive weren't coming, I served myself and sat next to Rose.

The room was silent as people munched sandwiches, staring into their plates. I suspected Marguerite was usually a more gracious hostess, but she nibbled at her salad, looking exhausted. They'd all been through a lot, first Hugh's death, and now a question of murder.

"Where are Vivian and Clive?" I asked.

Tallulah answered. "I dunno. Do you, Granny?"

"I do not." Marguerite didn't sound all that interested in finding out, either.

"How is your search for a new position progressing?" Marguerite asked Paolo.

"Nothing yet."

"Don't worry. Something will turn up soon, I'm sure."

"How did you and Paolo find each other?" Rose asked. "It turned out to be such a good thing for Hugh."

"For all of us," Marguerite responded. "Paolo worked for a friend of mine. Several friends, in fact. He came highly recommended."

That must be what life was like at Marguerite's great age. A constant round of friends needing hospice care for dying spouses, siblings, and themselves, even in Marguerite's tragic case for a child, or for someone she thought of as her child, even though he had once been someone else's.

The doorbell sounded, deep and resonant.

Marguerite sighed. "Vivian has forgotten her key once again."

"I'll get it," Rose said, but Jake was already on his feet.

He returned, followed by Detective Salinsky. "I told you I'd be back and I am," Salinsky said.

Marguerite spoke from the head of the table. "I hope you are here to tell us this silly business is over, and my son died of cancer, as we all expected."

"No," Salinsky responded. "I'm not. I'm here to tell you the medical examiner has determined Mr. Morales was murdered. I'll need to speak to each of you individually."

Chapter 21

Salinsky planned to talk to me last, or at least last of the people who were present. Vivian and Clive still hadn't turned up. I could see why the detective wanted to begin with the people who had been in the house when Hugh died.

After she finished her interview, I spent time in the kitchen with Rose preparing the lasagna. She focused on the task, mixing ricotta, Italian parsley, Romano cheese, and eggs in the food processor, while ground beef and onions sizzled in a deep frying pan on the stove.

"What did Detective Salinsky ask you?"

"What?" She cupped her ear, trying to hear over the frying meat and the *thrum* of the ancient stove fan.

After I repeated the question, she answered. "He asked about my medical practice. Hugh died twenty-four hours after a doctor arrived at the house. He asked about Hugh, and about everyone in the house."

"Does he know who Hugh really is?"

"Yes. That ship has sailed. Someone he interviewed before me must have told him, probably Marguerite."

Or he got there on his own. Salinsky would suspect someone in the house of the murder, wouldn't he, if in those last days Hugh couldn't leave and no one from the outside came to see him? I'd just found these people, and now all of them were murder suspects.

"Marguerite seems worn out by all this," I said.

"Can you blame her? First Hugh's illness and death and now the police and a murder," Rose responded.

"How is her health generally?"

Rose stopped working and looked at me. "Remarkably good, actually. That happens sometimes. If human beings get past the cancer years and then the heart disease years, then the dementia years, they can sometimes go on and on. Marguerite takes medication for high blood pressure, but that's quite recent. She could live for years, into her hundreds, possibly."

"I'd like my mom to meet her."

Rose gave my arm a squeeze. "I'm sure she will."

She put a giant roasting pan on the table and I helped her assemble the lasagna. She layered sauce, then noodles, the ricotta mixture, then the ground beef, then the Italian sausages she'd cooked in the sauce, then mozzarella.

She covered it all with a layer of sauce and we repeated the pattern.

"Where did you learn to make lasagna?"

"Med school roommate. My study group was always starving."

"Looks delicious."

After she put it in the oven, we chatted in low voices about our lives. She told me about her husband, who was also a physician, and her teenage son. I told her about the Snowden Family Clambake, and Chris, Mom, Livvie, Sonny, and Page.

At last there were footsteps on the stairs and Salinsky appeared in the kitchen doorway. "Your turn, Ms. Snowden."

I seated myself kitty-corner from him at the dining room table. He had dark hair flecked with white and bushy eyebrows. His whiskers were more noticeable than they had been earlier, and I wondered if he was the type of man who had to shave twice a day.

He flipped back through his handwritten notes, not speaking for a long time. I got more and more nervous. If Salinsky had checked me out through law enforcement databases, he wouldn't have found me there. But if he had done what I would have, and typed my name into a garden-variety search engine, he would have seen plenty of mentions of me in the Maine press, including the murder and a fire on Morrow Island in the spring and another corpse stowed in our clambake fire over the summer. I was not a murderer, but I had been murderer-adjacent all too many times.

I concentrated on breathing evenly. I hadn't killed my cousin Hugh. I hadn't known until after he was dead that he'd been alive the last thirty-some years.

Salinsky finally spoke. "When did you arrive in Boston, Ms. Snowden?"

"Yesterday evening."

"And you came straight here?"

"I checked into my hotel first." I gave him the details.

"What brought you to Boston?"

Well, that was the rub, wasn't it? I was perched on the razor's edge. If I didn't tell him about the Black Widow at this first opportunity, it would be infinitely more difficult to tell him later.

I didn't answer right away, and Salinsky went on. "Your mother was left a bequest in Hugh Morales's will—all of his personal property. Did you know he changed that will, adding your mother, just three months ago?"

"I didn't know about the will at all, until I got here."

Salinsky nodded and made a note. "Attorney Dickison has no doubt about the validity of the will. Mr. Morales was fully competent when he made it. By all reports, he was fully competent until he died. So I ask you again, what brought you here?"

It was do or die time. "A few days ago, someone sent a package to my mother."

"Someone?"

"I don't know who. There was no return address information. I didn't even know we had family in Boston. Or about Rose in California. Once we got the package, I tracked the family down."

"Must have been a pretty important package for you to do all that work and then travel here from Maine. What was in it?"

I took a deep breath. "A necklace. A diamond necklace with a large black diamond in the center, called the Black Widow."

"A large diamond? How large?"

"Seventy carats."

He whistled. "How much would something like that be worth?"

"I've had an estimate of around two million dollars."

He raised a bushy eyebrow at me. It was like a caterpillar wiggling across his forehead. "Two million dollars? No wonder you got in your boyfriend's truck and drove down here."

Boyfriend's truck? He'd already checked me out.

"So it wouldn't surprise you to know," he continued, "that Attorney Dickison is in possession of an inventory of Mr. Morales's personal property and it includes a diamond necklace valued at 2.25 million?"

I exhaled in a *whoosh.* I hadn't realized I'd been holding my breath. Thank goodness I'd told him the truth. "I wouldn't be surprised, no. But I'm kind of relieved. Until this moment I wasn't one hundred percent certain the necklace had come from Hugh."

"When did the package arrive, exactly?"

"Friday. At least, that's when Mom opened it. She hadn't picked up her mail for a couple of days because of the snow. The postmistress told me it was mailed on Tuesday."

"My understanding from everyone in the house is that Mr. Morales had not left the premises for some time before his death. Someone else must have sent it."

I nodded my agreement. "I've been trying to figure out who since I got here."

"You haven't told anyone in the house you have the necklace?"

"Not directly. I've asked a few people if Hugh had asked them to mail something."

Salinsky arranged his craggy features into a serious expression. "Excellent. Please don't mention the necklace to anyone."

"I won't. But why not? If the necklace is in Hugh's will they probably all know."

"It's not in the will. It's in an inventory of personal property no one in the family has seen. In my experience, wills changed shortly before death to favor unexpected beneficiaries can be a motive for murder." As he talked, he leaned across the table, bringing his face closer to mine. "Do you have any reason to suspect anyone in this house of murdering Hugh Morales?"

I hesitated. I didn't want to steer him wrong

and I had only suspicions. "I don't think Vivian's fiancé, Clive, is who or what he says he is."

Salinsky glanced at his notes. "And what does Mr. Humphries say he is? I haven't interviewed him yet. I'm told he lives here, but he's not at home this afternoon."

"He says he's an entrepreneur, trying to raise funds for a phone app, but he has absolutely no idea what he's talking about."

"And you base this impression on your years in venture capital, specifically in technology investment?"

He *had* checked me out. "I base it on my years of being a sentient human being."

Salinsky smiled. "I bet he wasn't happy to run into you."

"I don't think Clive knows my background. No one in the house seems to be aware of my recent past, except Rose." I left aside the topic of the scrapbook and how everyone in the house knew a creepy amount about my growing-up years.

Salinsky flipped through his notebook. "You may be interested to know that others have expressed doubts about Mr. Humphries, specifically, Mrs. Morales, Dr. Morrow, Tallulah Spencer, Jake Spencer, and Paolo Paolini."

"In other words, everyone you interviewed today."

He nodded. "Everyone presently at home. Mr. Humphries is not well liked, though being a fraud and being a murderer are two quite separate things."

"Hugh was so sick," I said. "How do you know he was murdered?"

"There are several indications that lead the medical examiner to that conclusion. There was an impression of your cousin's teeth on his upper lip, as if someone had pressed down hard on his face. There were goose feather particles and other textile matter in his airway. Hugh Morales was smothered with a bed pillow."

"But why? He was going to die, and soon."

Salinsky closed his notebook. "That's the question, isn't it? Who benefits by your cousin dying days before he otherwise would have?"

Chapter 22

After my interview, I found the others gathered in the living room, having well-deserved cocktails. The conversation died as soon as I entered the room. I was sure they'd been trading notes about their interviews with Salinsky. Their silence reminded me that though I was family, I was a stranger in their midst. The smell of Rose's lasagna bubbled up from the kitchen downstairs. My stomach growled so loudly they must have heard it. I poured a glass of wine. "Did we find out where Vivian and Clive are?" I asked.

"We were wondering whether to hold dinner for them when they called and asked us to wait," Marguerite answered. "They're on the way."

She'd no sooner said that than the door burst open and the sound of Vivian giggling came from the hall. "Oh, you silly boy." *Giggling? Had they been out in a bar?*

Vivian charged through the doorway into the living room, her left hand held out in front of her. Clive followed, still disentangling himself from his scarf.

"We got married!" Vivian crowed.

The reaction in the room was stunned silence.

"How? Where? Now?" Tallulah finally sputtered.

"By our friend who is a justice of the peace," Vivian said. "We got the license several days ago, but then Hugh died and the timing wasn't right."

"You thought better timing was the day before his memorial reception?" Tallulah's voice would have cut glass. "He's not even cremated."

"Nor likely to be soon," Paolo murmured.

"Don't be mad." Vivian stepped backward and took Clive's hand. "Before lunch, we got to talking. Life is short, as Hugh's death proves. We need to grab what happiness we can. There was no reason to delay and every reason to go forward." She stopped and looked around the room. "Isn't anyone going to offer congratulations?"

Jake raised his glass. "I know what Hugh would have said. 'My dear cousin Vivian.'" He imitated the voice I'd never heard. "'I wish you every happiness, as I have wished it for you six times before.'"

Only Tallulah laughed out loud. Rose and

Paolo suppressed smiles. Marguerite didn't seem capable of finding amusement in the subject.

Vivian poured wine for both herself and Clive. She raised her glass. "Thank you, Jake, for channeling Hugh's best wishes, which, by the way, would have been sincere."

We all raised our glasses, offering tepid congratulations, while Marguerite struggled to her feet. "Let's dine, shall we? I'm famished."

I thought the meal might be saved by Rose's delicious lasagna. It was like heaven in a pasta bowl, piquant with tomatoes, sweet with sausage, savory with cheese, and warm and comforting on a winter night. Rose served it with a simple salad of greens, oil, vinegar, and herbs, and a loaf of Italian bread, loaded with butter and garlic.

Even Marguerite seemed momentarily buoyed by the deliciousness. "This is so good. It reminds me of a lasagna I had in Rome in 1957. One would think you were Italian, dear Rose." Rose smiled, pleased by the compliment. Marguerite went on. "You've been too kind, caring for the family while you've been here."

"It's the least I can do to help out. I loved Uncle Hugh, and I've loved coming here all these years. You're the only family I've got left."

"I suppose after the memorial reception is over, you'll be leaving us?" Vivian suggested.

"Soon," Rose said. "Though I haven't booked my ticket yet."

Vivian turned to Paolo. "And how long will we be graced with your presence?"

Paolo blushed and stuttered slightly. "Mrs. Morales said I could stay until I find my next job. Since I am living here, I have no place to go until I am working again."

Vivian put down her fork. "How inconvenient. For us, that is."

"Enough," Marguerite said. "Paolo will come with us to the reception for Hugh tomorrow. There will be plenty of people there with an interest in his services."

Vivian nodded. "If your friends turn out, Mother, it will be a veritable convention of the halt and the lame. Paolo could stand on the front stoop of the Harvard Club and wait for someone to slip down it."

"I only work with the terminally ill," Paolo corrected. "I am a trained hospice—"

"And you." Vivian turned to me. "You'll be leaving town after the memorial reception as well?"

I didn't want to go. I hadn't figured out who had sent the Black Widow to Mom yet. Or why. But I had to get back to running the restaurant. And Livvie was due any moment. I realized with a pang that I hadn't checked in with Mom since her call at lunchtime. "My boyfriend is flying into Logan on Saturday," I answered. "I'll leave with him." I would run out of hotel points before then, and would have to charge my room to a credit card I had no immediate prospects of paying off, but that was a small investment in the face of two million dollars.

Marguerite smiled. "Rose and Julia, you are always welcome here. You must think of this as your ancestral home. Julia, you will move here from your hotel tomorrow morning."

"I . . ." The invitation surprised me. We'd met for the first time twenty-four hours earlier. But it seemed very like Marguerite to want us all under the same roof. Of course, if Salinsky was correct, one person under this roof was a murderer, who might have been motivated by the diamond necklace sitting in the safe deposit box in Busman's Harbor.

Clive had said nothing through the meal, eating little and pounding down red wine. His complexion had grown ruddier, his chin closer to his plate. "Well, not *always* welcome here," he said.

That was a conversation stopper. Everyone looked at him.

"What do you mean?" Tallulah's voice shook.

He looked up from his plate, all innocence. "What's the matter? If this week has taught us anything, it's that no one lives forever. Not even you, Marguerite." He looked from Marguerite to Tallulah. "And when Marguerite is gone, you can expect some changes in *our* house."

Rose gasped. Tallulah's mouth fell open. Paolo clenched his fists on the table. Even Jake, who seemed like the nicest guy in the world, looked like he wanted to punch somebody. One particular somebody.

"Stop it," Marguerite commanded. "I, and I alone will decide who is welcome here. Paolo and Rose stay, and Julia will move her things over in the morning. This is still my house. I'm not dead yet." She wiped her mouth with a red cloth napkin. "You will never be the owner of this home," she said to Clive, emphasizing each word so he couldn't miss the meaning. "And neither will Vivian, who has this once and final time proved herself too . . . too imbecilic to handle the responsibility. After the memorial, I will speak to Mr. Dickison about leaving the house, along with the money Hugh provided to run it, directly to Tallulah."

Vivian stood up. "You'll never get away with it, you sad, old bat. I'll have you declared incompetent. I'll speak to a lawyer too. You've dedicated your life to thwarting me, making sure I never got anything I wanted." Vivian's voice had risen throughout the tirade and by the end she was shouting. "Clive, come along. We're going upstairs." She looked back at her mother. "It is our honeymoon."

Marguerite rose on unsteady legs. "Vivian, when will you learn that to hurt me, there is no need to hurt yourself?"

Vivian shot her mother a look of pure hatred, and then she and Clive bolted out of the dining room.

Tallulah was on her feet as well. She pointed at me. "If you came here to find family, this is it. Welcome to our happy home." She rushed from the room too, with Jake following. From below, those of us who remained heard first one bedroom door, and then another, slam.

Marguerite sat back down. "Rose, I apologize for the way my family has treated your wonderful meal. Let's finish up and then repair to the living room for a brandy."

Chapter 23

We finished the meal without speaking, the forks scraping the bottoms of our pasta bowls the only sound. Paolo insisted on cleaning up. "You have done more than enough," he said to Rose.

Marguerite lingered in the dining room while Rose and I helped Paolo clear the table, the three of us moving from dining room to kitchen, up and down the stairs. The basement kitchen was traditional and charming, but it was a real pain in the neck.

"There should be a dumbwaiter," I said to Rose as we passed each other on the stairs, carrying plates, glasses, and cutlery.

"I believe we are the dumb waiters." She smiled.

Paolo washed the dishes, and Rose and I escorted Marguerite into the living room. Three full snifters of brandy sat on a silver tray on the table next to Marguerite's chair.

"How lovely. Who did this for us?" Marguerite went for the chair and reached for the nearest glass.

"Not me," I answered.

"Me either," Rose said. "Paolo must have done it while Julia and I were clearing. Let me." Rose picked up the tray. She passed a snifter to Marguerite and brought the tray to me.

"I shouldn't." I'd had a glass of wine before dinner and another with the meal.

"Oh, pish. Live a little," Marguerite urged. "Before bed, drink a large glass of water to prevent a hangover. I always keep a glass by my bed for just that purpose. Don't they teach young ladies anything anymore?"

I took the snifter. Rose put the last one on the table next to her chair and returned the tray to its place.

"I'm sorry about the scene in the dining room," Marguerite said.

I was no stranger to family drama. When your family works together every day and all depend on money coming out of the same pot, the stakes are high and the arguments can get heated. Sonny and I, in particular, had our issues. He'd resented me coming home to run the clambake and had fought every change I'd tried to make to rescue the business. I, in turn, had failed to honor his respect for tradition, including the traditions that had made the clambake successful in the first place. We'd worked it all out in the end, but our personalities were so opposite, I was certain we'd clash again in the future.

"How is your boy?" Marguerite asked Rose.

Rose smiled, eyes crinkling, obviously proud. "He's a wonderful son. Kind and generous. Tall and handsome, like his father. He's a National Merit Scholar, in the model UN. He wants to be a diplomat."

"Not a doctor like his parents?"

"No, but that's fine. He has to follow his own path."

"You must miss him a great deal."

"I do." Rose's smile faded. "But I'm grateful he's old enough that I was able to spend this time with you and Hugh."

"We're grateful too." Marguerite assured her. "You're parenting well. I envy you. Vivian is my great failure."

Rose and I turned our attention to her fully. I was dying to know what she thought, specifically, her failure had been, but I couldn't think of a way to ask the question.

Fortunately, she went on. "I don't know where I failed her, but you see the results. My mother was strict. I rebelled and rebelled. I dropped out of my senior year of boarding school, married a man I barely knew, and went off to Spain to fight Franco. I was a fervent supporter of the republic and a sworn enemy of fascism, but as I look back, it was all about getting away from my mother." She frowned, the web of wrinkles around her mouth deepening. "I saw things no human should ever see because I was less afraid of war than I was of telling off my mother. I tried to be more lenient with Vivian, more supportive of her dreams. You see the result."

I'd been the dutiful child in my family, cooperatively excelling at boarding school, college, and business school, while Livvie insisted she wanted nothing in the world but to graduate from Busman's High, marry Sonny Ramsey, and have his baby. She flunked out of so many prep schools my parents gave up. Then, during her senior year, she announced she was pregnant. I'd seen myself as the mature one and Livvie as the stubborn, immature rebel. But now that I'd been back home in Busman's Harbor for a year, I saw it as the reverse. At sixteen, Livvie knew exactly what she wanted, while I had floated along, molded by my parents' expectations.

"Sometimes a little rebellion is a good thing," I said.

Marguerite sighed. "I'm sure you're right. I thought I had given her no reason, but Vivian has rebelled against me again and again, always in the same way—by marrying unsuitable men. By marrying the same unsuitable man, over and over, truth be told. Men who are parasites, every single one of them. Even my dear Tallulah's father was a leech who hung on to its host for his entire life. We've paid every one of them to go away. The amount of money that's been flushed down the drain on Vivian's husbands is unconscionable. It's depleted me."

"And now there's Clive Humphries," Rose said.

"As worthless as the others. It's a pattern I fear she cannot break. Vivian can't be without a man, a man who pays attention and flatters her. Then, after they move into the house and marry, they can never pay her enough attention. She grows frustrated and desperate. They, in turn, stay away, or more often stray away. Soon we are paying for another divorce."

"You could ask the happy couple to live somewhere else," Rose suggested.

"I have, occasionally, though they always return. Neither Vivian nor these men have any ability to make a living." Marguerite finished her brandy with a gulp. "The last two figured they could outlast me and inherit, but I've defied them by living to my great old age. I'm sure that's what Clive means to do as well, especially with Hugh no longer with us. But I'll never let that happen."

"Tallulah and Jake are a good match," Rose pointed out. "She doesn't seem to have her mother's romantic impulsiveness."

Marguerite smiled. "They are well suited, aren't they? They married too young—I was against it. But that's often the way with children from unstable homes. They are driven to create family. At least Tallulah chose wisely. I thought Jake was too laid back for her, too easily pushed around, but he's been a tremendous stabilizing influence. It does my old heart well to see them together." Marguerite shifted in her chair, and shifted the subject as well. "Julia, it's time for you to tell us about your branch of the family. You run a clambake on Morrow Island."

I nodded enthusiastically. "The Snowden Family Clambake. We have a tour boat and twice a day during the summer season we give tourists a harbor tour and then bring them to Morrow Island for a real Maine clambake."

"Pardon my West Coast ignorance," Rose said. "But what is a real Maine clambake?"

Marguerite answered, eyes twinkling. "Chowder, twin lobsters, steamed clams, corn on the cob, a potato, and an onion, cooked over a hardwood fire, and under seaweed and sailcloth tarps wet down with salt water."

"And an egg," I added, a particular spin of our family.

"An egg?" Rose asked.

"The eggs go on top of the pile. An egg is removed and opened. If it is hard cooked, the rest of the food is done."

"Sounds wonderful," Rose said.

"You must come." I meant it.

"But isn't it hard having all those strangers running all over the island?" Marguerite asked.

"The Snowden Family Clambake is all I have ever known. It's normal to me." While it was true that we locked the little house on the island to guard against marauding strangers, they were usually guests who were lost and looking for the restroom, easily turned around and sent in the right direction.

I thought about the sepia photo I'd gotten from the historical society. So much of the beauty of Morrow Island had been sacrificed over the years. Woods had replaced the rose garden, and a warren of buildings, including the dining pavilion, kitchen, bar, and gift shop, occupied the great lawn. But the idea the business had destroyed the island was absurd. My parents had founded and worked their tails off at the Snowden Family Clambake in order to keep Morrow Island in the family.

"And then you had that terrible fire last summer," Marguerite said, while Rose nodded knowingly. "Such a shame."

They knew because of the scrapbook. They'd known about and dissected the public part of my family's lives for decades, while we didn't know they existed. My resentment boiled over. "Why did Hugh do it?" I demanded. "Why did he never contact my mother?"

They both shook their heads. Finally, Marguerite spoke. "He never said why. I urged him to contact her many times, just as in the early years I begged him to tell his parents. He wouldn't. He hated his parents. But that wasn't the case with your mother."

"He only spoke of her with fondness," Rose said. "With love."

There was a moment of quiet, each of us lost in our own thoughts. I longed to tell these lovely women that Mom had the Black Widow, and ask them about it directly, but I'd promised Detective Salinsky I wouldn't, so I let it go.

"Your mother should come to Hugh's memorial reception tomorrow," Marguerite said. "Now that he's gone, there's nothing to prevent the rest of us from meeting her."

There were several things preventing it, chief among them that I hadn't yet told Mom Hugh had been alive all those years.

"Julia's sister Livvie is having a baby at any moment," Rose explained.

"A baby, how lovely. It makes me feel better about Hugh's passing to see the family go on." Marguerite raised her empty snifter. "To new life coming in. My invitation is sincere," she said to me. "I want you to move into the house tomorrow." She put down her glass and reached for her cane.

"I'm overwhelmed. That's so generous."

"I insist." It seemed like she was used to getting her way when she insisted.

"Thank you." On the one hand, I'd be moving into a house that might hold a murderer. On the other, staying with the family might get me the information I needed about who had sent the Black Widow, and who owned it. I couldn't turn that down. "I'll bring my things in the morning."

Chapter 24

Back in my hotel room, I stared at my phone. No messages from Chris, which galled me after his remark that he had no reason to stay in Maine in the winter. I imagined him, drinking beer at a noisy tropical bar full of scantily clad women, while I froze my patooties off and dug through the mother of all family dysfunction.

I shook myself out of my self-pity and did what I had to do. I called my mother. The time had come to tell her what was really going on. I couldn't explain to her how she owned the Black Widow if I didn't explain whom she'd inherited it from, or how Hugh had been alive all these years she'd believed he was dead. The weight of the secret was unsettling me. The longer I kept it, the more I was a coconspirator like the rest of them, perpetuating this awful hoax on my mother.

"Mom, it's me. Where are you?"

"I'm at Livvie's." In the background, I heard

the sound of the giant television Sonny's dad had given the family. My sister hated it. "She's resting." Mom answered my question, even though I hadn't asked it.

"Good. Mom, you might want to go to your room and shut the door for this conversation."

"Julia, you're making me nervous." The noise of the TV receded. I heard a door close and pictured Mom sitting on the miserable pullout couch in Livvie's guest room. "Go ahead."

I took a deep breath and told her everything. From the moment I told her about Hugh, she cried—great, heaving sobs echoing through the air, transmitted satellite to satellite.

"Why?" she asked over and over. "Why, why, why?"

I waited for her to compose herself. "I don't know why. I'm not sure anyone does. The way Marguerite tells it, his disappearance was something of an accident."

"An accident? How could anything like that have been an accident?"

"He told her he had an argument with a girl and hid on the boat. Do you remember an argument, or a girl, for that matter?"

Mom didn't say anything. Her intermittent sniffing told me she was trying to get control. "No," she finally said. "Nothing like that." Then she dissolved again. "I don't understand."

I told her what Marguerite had said about Hugh's hatred for his parents. I reassured her that both Paolo and Rose said he talked of her fondly and often at the end. I didn't mention the scrapbook. It was too obsessive and creepy.

That he remembered her in his final days brought back the tears. "I don't understand why he would have done this. I loved him like a brother."

I talked to her until she calmed down. I told her about the town house that had been owned by her ancestors and described the family members, giving the best spin I could.

After we hung up, I was remorseful about the pain I'd caused her. *You didn't cause it, Hugh did*, I told myself. There had been no avoiding the conversation.

It was only then I realized Mom had not asked one thing about the necklace.

I was too keyed up to sleep. I fired up my laptop and searched for information about Clive Humphries. He had a profile on LinkedIn, though I didn't recognize the names of five most recent employers he'd listed on his résumé. I entered a couple of the company names in a search engine and found nothing. The GimmeThat! App had a web site, but, as I expected, it was a mile wide, an inch deep, and said nothing.

Rose, I knew from my previous searches, was exactly what she seemed, a well-respected doctor in San Francisco. I realized belatedly I'd forgotten to ascertain Vivian's last name immediately prior to her marriage to Clive, so I figured I'd start at the beginning. I typed "Vivian Morales," and was lucky enough to score a full wedding article from the *Globe*. Vivian's marriage to husband number one had been big news back in 1981. Then came number two, then three, who was presumably Tallulah's father. I wondered if he was still in Tallulah's life, until I found an obituary for him in 2011. After him came wedding announcements four, five, and six, though smaller and smaller notices.

Tallulah Spencer was easy to find on the Internet. She and her accompanist, Jake Spencer, performed at clubs in Boston and Cambridge as well as other places around New England, just as Rose had said.

So far, I hadn't learned anything helpful, but I decided to keep going, just to check all the boxes. I typed "Paolo Paolini Boston," and got nothing. Absolutely nothing. Would a hospice nurse necessarily have a web presence? It was hard to avoid nowadays, unless the obscurity was intentional. Perhaps he was undocumented. Or he had some other, more sketchy reason for staying in the shadows. I'd make an effort to find out more in the morning.

I climbed into bed and closed my eyes, but sleep didn't come. I felt terrible about what I'd had to tell my mother. It was so hurtful. Hugh's disappearance had haunted her life. Why had he done that to her? The question pinged around my brain. *Stop it,* I finally ordered. *You need to sleep. Tomorrow is going to be another long day.*

Just as I drifted off, my chest contracted, as if it was being squeezed by a giant's hand. I gulped for air, unable to breathe.

I'd had panic attacks before. Toward the end of my career in venture capital, they'd become almost chronic, though I'd only had two since I'd moved back to Busman's Harbor. But something was off about this one. I couldn't get a breath, but my heart wasn't racing, my brain wasn't darting off in a million anxiety-filled directions. A massive lethargy overcame me. I didn't have enough energy left to panic.

I focused on what was happening. Had I suddenly developed some kind of asthma? An allergy to the feathers the hotel claimed were in my pillows and comforter? Or was it something I'd eaten or drunk? I catalogued the amount I'd had to drink. It was a lot for me, far more than usual, but I'd consumed it over hours, and I hadn't felt drunk or even tipsy on my walk back to the hotel or anytime since.

I couldn't get my mind off those full snifters of brandy. Rose had concluded Paolo had filled them, and it was likely he had, slipping into the living room while Marguerite was in the dining room and Rose and I climbed up and down the stairs clearing the table.

Paolo was a stranger in the house. He didn't exist on the web. Could he have put something in my drink? But why?

I worried about Marguerite and Rose. What

if their drinks were also doctored? I debated whether to call. A phone call to the Marlborough Street house in the middle of the night would distress everyone, and I wasn't sure what was happening to me. What would I say? My mind was so muddled, I couldn't think it through.

Exerting an effort, I raised my arm off the bed and picked up the receiver of the hotel phone. I waited, hand poised over the operator button, ready to sound the alarm if I felt I was going to pass out.

The feeling like I had a steel band around my chest, while the rest of my muscles had turned to jelly, continued, but it didn't get worse. The minutes ticked by, then turned to a quarter hour, then an hour. Finally around 2:00 AM, the constriction eased. I took a breath, then a deeper breath. The sensation had been like none I'd ever felt before.

I pushed to a sitting position, then swung my heavy legs over the side of the bed. I opened the curtains and looked at the cityscape. Boston was quiet, much quieter than New York would have been at the same hour, but there were cars and cabs and delivery trucks in the street below. Across the Charles, headlights and taillights moved along a curving road. I walked the attack off, growing stronger and steadier. Convinced whatever had happened was over, I picked up my book and read until my eyes finally closed, around three.

Chapter 25

The lobby was nearly deserted in the morning. The clerk assured me Chris's truck could stay in the hotel garage for an extortionate fee until I was ready to leave the city. I wheeled my carry-on-sized bag out onto the sidewalk.

I felt fine. The scary episode the night before must have been one of my usual panic attacks combined with a fair amount of alcohol and an overstimulated imagination.

People passed me, hurrying to their destinations. When I got to the corner of Marlborough and Dartmouth streets, I stood for a moment looking at Marguerite's town house. Which window framed the room that would be mine? All the rooms on the second floor were occupied, so I assumed I'd be on the third, tucked under the mansard roof.

Before I could get to the front door, Clive stepped onto the stoop. He lit a cigarette and inhaled deeply. "Hullo. Don't tell."

"Of course not," I answered as I climbed the front steps. "Your secret is safe with me."

The color drained from his handsome face. "What secret? Why would you think I have a secret?"

Which of his many secrets was he worried about? That he wasn't who he said he was? That his app was a scam? Or, that he'd married Vivian for her money, perhaps a pointless effort if Marguerite found a way to cut him out. "Clive, you just told me you have a secret. You asked me to keep the smoking quiet."

"Yeah, well." He recovered himself. "Sorry. I'm a little off. It's crazy in there." He inclined his head to indicate the inside of the town house. "Everyone's getting dressed, fighting over the bathrooms." Clive looked down at the front of his snappy, charcoal-colored overcoat. "We've all got to look our best for old Hugh."

"Paolo told me you read to him."

"We all did. It was Hugh's favorite way to pass the time, aside from napping, which he did a lot toward the end."

"That was nice of you. Is everyone okay today?" I wanted to ask if anyone had stopped breathing in the night.

"Physically or mentally?" Clive answered my question with a joke.

"Today's reception will be difficult for the entire family." It wasn't a day for joking.

He took a long drag. "My take with these WASPs is they'll act like it's a normal cocktail party on a normal day. They're not big on public displays of emotion."

If Clive Humphries wasn't a WASPy name, I didn't know what was. Perhaps "Clive" needed to remember more carefully who he was pretending to be.

Clive stubbed out his cigarette on the stone railing. "I hope there are some new prospects at this shindig I can pitch on GimmeThat!"

I played along. "Hugh's friends must have money."

He grunted. "Realtors. They invest in things they can see, touch, live, or work in. They're not interested in tech. Besides, I already tried most of them as they came by the house to see Hugh near the end."

I shuddered, thinking of Clive at the bottom of the stairs, buttonholing Hugh's grieving visitors. "What about Vivian's friends?"

Clive scoffed. Not many people can scoff, but Clive carried it off. "Already tried them too. I had one on the line, but her son got wind and put a stop to it. 'She's not a sophisticated investor. She doesn't belong in something so risky.' You know the drill."

I didn't. I knew about raising money for new businesses, but not doing it the way Clive operated. A gust of wind cut through my down coat. "Let's go inside," I suggested.

Clive opened the door and held it, like the gentleman he most definitely was not.

* * *

Marguerite was in the front hall, looking perfectly fit for a ninety-six-year-old. "You're here." She moved forward and took both my gloved hands.

"How are you?" I asked. "How did you sleep?"

"Quite well," she answered. "Considering everything." She gave a tilt of her head that indicated everything—Hugh's death, the murder investigation, and Vivian's marriage. Then, she called to Jake, who was in the living room. "Take Julia to her room so she can get settled. One of the center rooms on the third floor. They're both made up."

Jake and I chatted amiably as I followed him up the stairs. He was a likable guy, an easygoing presence in a house full of people who were anything but.

On the third floor, the ceilings were low, the rooms small and obviously meant for servants. In my room, a single bed was pushed against the wall and a naked lightbulb hung from the ceiling. Cracks spider-webbed across the dingy paint and discoloration from an old leak marked the ceiling.

Jake put down my suitcase. "Paolo's in the room at the back, and Clive's at the front."

"Clive is?"

Jake let out a soft laugh. "Marguerite's a stickler for propriety, I'm afraid. The room next to you was mine until my wedding." He flashed his left hand with the simple gold band on his ring finger. "Of course, most nights, Marguerite goes to bed by ten, so she doesn't know what happens after that. I did have some close calls when I was sneaking out of Tallulah's room in the morning. I guess Clive will officially move down to Vivian's room now that they're married." He looked at the old-fashioned alarm clock on the bureau. "I'd better get dressed."

At the door, he lingered. "I'm sorry about the scene in the dining room last night. Lulah's not normally like that, but she's broken up about Hugh. Her dad was never in the picture, and her mom's attention is sporadic, best case. Marguerite and Hugh were really her parents, in terms of what you'd expect from parents— consistency, stability, encouragement. Lulah's had a lot to be sad about."

"I'm sorry. I wish I had known Hugh."

"You missed someone special."

Not by my choice.

He turned to go. "Lunch is at one and the cars pick us up at two."

When Jake was gone, I sat on the bed for a moment to decompress. I had no intention of unpacking. I wasn't going to stay long.

I changed out of my jeans into the same skirt and top I'd worn the day before, the only decent clothes I'd brought. I found the bathroom down the hall, over the one on the second floor, and even less improved. The toilet had a pull chain that hung from a box high on the wall, and the shower was a jury-rigged tangle of plumbing over the claw-foot tub.

I returned to my room, thinking about the town house. The Black Widow was worth two-plus million dollars, but Marguerite's house had to be worth five times that. Its gently crumbling state wouldn't deter a developer who would reno and condo it.

There was a soft rap on the door. When I called, "Come in," it swung gently open and Paolo appeared. He was dressed in a sport coat and a crisply ironed shirt. He looked sharp and not at all sinister. "I stopped in on my way downstairs to see if there is anything you need."

"Thanks. Is there a Wi-Fi password?" I asked, the very definition of disingenuous.

"No, no such conveniences. Mr. Clive uses the network of one of the neighbors. I myself do not use the Internet."

"You don't use the Internet at all? Don't you work with an agency that places you? How do you find jobs?"

He shook his head. "No agency. Word of mouth from client to client. An exclusive group looking for something particular. I have been lucky in my placements."

That seemed odd to me. Could he really be employed full-time by personal recommendations only? "You told me Hugh never asked you to mail a package to my mother, and I believe you. But I think you know something about that package, or the reason it was sent." I didn't know if he would respond. I wasn't even sure he knew anything, really.

Eventually, he spoke. "In the last weeks, Mr.

Hugh was unable to leave his room. As you will
have heard, the family came in. Sometimes they
talked, and most often they read to him. I left
them alone with him. Toward the end, Mr. Hugh
slept more frequently. Often they could read
only a few pages before he dropped off."

I nodded, hoping Paolo would go on. His
forehead twitched. He took a deep breath. "I
noticed that both Mrs. Vivian and Mrs. Tallulah
searched his room. Drawers were left pulled forward. Books rearranged on the shelves. Small
things, but when you spend as many hours in a
room as I did that one, you know when something has been moved."

"Vivian and Tallulah searched the room sep-
arately?"

"It is funny that you ask that. I believe they
both did, but not at the same time. First Vivian,
then when she stopped, Tallulah. Then when
Tallulah stopped, Vivian started again, only
more frantic this time. She left things about. Mr.
Hugh was even more often sleeping, less and
less wakeful. It was like she didn't think he
would notice or she didn't care."

"When was this?"

"It started two weeks before Mr. Hugh died.
The last time Vivian searched his room was the
day before he died. She may even have searched
it after. I am less frequently there, now that
Mr. Hugh has passed. I know everything in
the room was supposed to go to your mother.
I'm sorry if something you expected to be
there is missing."

I had expected nothing. Nor had my mother. She thought Hugh had been dead for all these years. "What did you do about this searching, if anything?" I asked.

"When I first suspected Vivian, I told Mr. Hugh. I said, 'She looks for something.' He said he would take care of it. After that conversation, Vivian came and searched again. I mentioned it to Mr. Hugh again. He told me not to worry. So I didn't. There were many things to attend to by then, so I let it go."

Chapter 26

I helped Rose put the leftover sandwiches from the previous day on the table for lunch. "Did you sleep well?" I asked.

"Like a baby. That's what a late-night brandy will do for you."

The household gathered, but only Jake ate more than a nibble. The conversation was limited to "Please pass me the—" and "Thank you." Everyone seemed to be doing his or her best to forget the scene from the night before and to prepare themselves for the next few hours, when they'd have to maintain their public faces while receiving condolences about Hugh.

The cars arrived and we departed. Paolo and Jake helped Marguerite down the treacherous front walk. Vivian put herself, Marguerite, Tallulah, and Clive in the first car and Jake, Rose, Paolo, and me in the second. Clearly we were the B group.

We drove a short distance and stopped outside

a solid brick building with flags fluttering in the wind. I understood why at ninety-six Marguerite had needed a ride, but the rest of us could have easily walked. Actually, given the vagaries of Boston's one-way streets, traffic jams, jaywalkers, and kamikaze bike riders, we could have more easily walked than driven.

The driver of the town car jumped out and opened the rear door. He waved off the tip Jake offered. "Already taken cah of," he said in a thick Boston accent. "I'll be back to pick you up at fo-ah." He looked toward the sky. "If you'd like me to come earlia, call. Ms. Morales has the numba."

Inside the Harvard Club, a solicitous employee showed us to the room Marguerite had reserved for the occasion. I gathered she was a well-known guest, especially given the number of servers and others who approached her to say how sorry they were about Mr. Morales. As we walked down the hall, I thought about all the business deals done, the fortunes made and lost in these rooms across three different centuries, including our own.

We stood for a moment, staring at one another, and then there were voices in the hallway and wave after wave of people entered. We had formed a semicircle, not a receiving line exactly, but to make it easy for guests to greet the family as they came in. I didn't know a soul, but Marguerite kept me firmly by her side, insisting I be introduced to everyone.

Hugh's real estate friends were buttoned

down and sleek, in well-tailored suits, both the men and the women. Tallulah and Jake's friends were young and scruffy. I wondered what Marguerite made of the piercings and the body jewelry. Tallulah had covered her tattoo for the occasion, though she'd stuck with her usual heavy eye makeup. Her friends shuffled in, muttered "sorry about your uncle," and went in search of the bar. I noticed Marguerite shaking her head, but their behavior wasn't that different than the "so, so sorrys" and air-kisses of Vivian's friends.

Vivian's friends I recognized. They were the clubwomen and the volunteers, like the mothers of my prep school classmates. They were the kind of women who knew how things should be done and made sure they were done that way.

They were all women. Admittedly, it was 2:00 o'clock in the afternoon on a Wednesday, but my work experience told me the kinds of men these women would be married to could get away from the office in the middle of the day if they needed to. The men didn't come, I assumed, because they didn't want to, because they didn't think it was important. Or, because there were no men—no husbands, partners, lovers, boyfriends. Vivian was a serial marryer. Maybe these were the women she returned to after each one ended. Her real tribe.

Vivian waved the ring Clive had "bought" her under their noses. Her announcement was met with shrieks and good wishes, so different from its reception at home. She didn't seem to care about stealing the focus of the afternoon from Hugh. Tallulah stood with her cluster of friends and glared at her mother.

Clive had no friends, or at least none who thought it was important to show up for his wife's cousin's memorial reception. He leaned against the wall, champagne flute in hand.

I didn't get the format of the event. Would someone—Marguerite, Tallulah, one of the friends—say some words about Hugh? But as Clive had predicted, everyone went about their business as if it was a normal cocktail party on a normal day, as if cocktail parties were normally held at two in the afternoon on a Wednesday. In the conversations around me, I heard snatches of reminiscences about Hugh, and conversations beginning, "When did you see him last?" But no one made a move to do anything more formal.

I spotted Paolo standing alone on the other side of the room and walked toward him. As I reached him, another woman strode purposely forward. "Paolo! How wonderful to see you." She was a skinny woman dressed in a dark eggplant-colored suit. Her white hair was neatly coiffed, but from the rest of her it was impossible to tell how old she was or to guess if she was a friend of Vivian's or Marguerite's. She gave Paolo a tight hug, closing her eyes as if savoring the closeness. "It's been too long."

Paolo stepped politely out of the embrace. "How have you been, Mrs. Hoover?"

Her expression sobered. "Honestly, I have good days and bad. I miss Mom terribly, but her suffering is over. I'm so glad I was able to keep her in her home until the end. Thanks to you." She turned to me and held out her hand. "I'm Claire Hoover, and you are—?"

"Ah, excuse me," Paolo said. "This is Julia Snowden. She is a cousin to Mr. Morales."

Claire Hoover shook my hand. "So nice to meet more family. I didn't see you at the house when Hugh was ill."

Where to even start? I hadn't visited Hugh when he was sick because I thought he'd been dead longer than I'd been alive.

"Ms. Snowden lives in Maine," Paolo said, as if that explained everything. Thankfully, for Claire it did.

"I must tell you what a wonder this man is," she said, grasping Paolo's forearm. "He was a saint with my mother, an absolute saint. He made her final days so joyful and comfortable. The whole family got to say their good-byes. My only regret . . ." She paused and her eyes filled with tears. The loss seemed deep and recent. "My only regret is that no one was with her when she died. But we had all seen her that day. She had a few more days on earth at best. I'm at peace with it."

Paolo's eyes slid from one side to the other. He took my arm. "I think we must talk to others. The family will be waiting."

"You go ahead," I said. "I'll catch up."

He turned reluctantly away. There was no way he could force me to move.

"When did your mother pass away?" I asked in a tone I hoped conveyed caring concern, not rabid curiosity.

"Two months ago. It was expected. She was quite elderly and suffered from heart failure and the beginnings of dementia. She died right before Marguerite brought Hugh home from the hospital the last time. The fortunate thing was the timing. When Marguerite called, I was able to recommend Paolo unreservedly, and happy that he found a new job so quickly. I suppose he's looking now. I'll try to think of any friends who might be in need."

"How did you find Paolo?"

"From the Jenkinses. They're here somewhere. Rita is in our book group with Marguerite and me."

"Can you introduce me? I'd like to meet some of Cousin Marguerite's friends."

"Of course."

It took only a few minutes with the Jenkinses, a husband and wife in late middle age, to discover that Paolo had cared for Mr. Jenkins's father, who'd had a devastating stroke and then lingered for months. They spoke glowingly of the role Paolo had played in their household at the end of the senior Mr. Jenkins's life.

"Were you with him when he died?" It was an inappropriate question, and somewhat out of the blue from a total stranger.

The Jenkinses didn't seem to notice. "He passed away peacefully in his sleep," Mr. Jenkins answered. "The night after my brother arrived from South Africa and had a chance to say good-bye. It was terrible. Dad lingered those last months after the stroke," Mr. Jenkins said. "But he went, quietly, alone, without fuss, as he would have wanted."

"Who recommended Paolo to you?" I asked.

"Mrs. Price." Mrs. Jenkins pointed to an elderly woman seated in a chair against the wall. She hadn't removed her overcoat and clutched her handbag as if she was on the street in the roughest part of town instead of at the Harvard Club. "Paolo cared for her husband during his final illness." Mr. and Mrs. Jenkins both looked over at Mrs. Price. "Poor woman. I don't think she's gotten over his death."

"Can you introduce me?"

By the time I'd finished talking to Mrs. Price, I was certain of what I had heard. "He was in so much pain," Mrs. Price said. "He held on until our golden wedding anniversary. He was more lucid that day than he'd been in months. At midnight, we toasted. I fed him some champagne through a straw and left him. By morning, he was gone."

Three cases, or four if you counted Hugh's, where a terminally ill person had died, "expectedly, but unexpectedly," immediately after the arrival of a loved one, or some other important milestone was passed. No one regarded the deaths as suspicious, like no one in the town house regarded Hugh's death as suspicious. Except for the person who had called the police.

Paolo had tracked me around the room with his eyes, though he never approached me. When I saw his back was turned, I scurried out of the function room and ducked into the coatroom across the hall. I pulled the business card Salinksy had left the first day from my bag and turned my phone on. I noticed four calls from Chris, spaced about twenty minutes apart. I'd have to get back to him too. I called Salinsky first.

"Detective Salinsky, Boston Police Department, Homicide," he answered.

"This is Julia Snowden, Hugh Morales's cousin."

"Ah, the mysterious heir."

"Yes, that's me. Or actually my mother is the heir. I need to speak to you as soon as possible. There is someone I strongly suspect in Hugh Morales's murder. I need to tell you who it is and why. I want to do it face to face."

"Where are you?"

"At the Harvard Club in Back Bay."

"Is the person you suspect there with you?"

"Yes. And I'd prefer not to make a fuss here. It's a reception in Hugh's memory. I don't want to disrupt it."

"I'm at the precinct. Come to the front desk

and ask for me." He gave me the address and ended the call. I turned to leave the coatroom and heard a snuffle. Great, someone had overheard me. "Hullo? Who's here?"

"It's me." Tallulah stepped out from behind a rack of coats, eyes red, nose running. The heavy eye makeup she always wore ran down her cheeks.

"What's the matter?" She looked so miserable, I stepped forward to embrace her. "I know you loved Hugh."

She sniffed again, stepped back, and blotted her nose with a tissue. "It's not that. I mean, I miss Hugh and all, but that's not it." She threw her hand outward in a gesture of despair. "I hate my mother. I hate her. I hate her."

I put the best spin I could on it. "Perhaps she's mourning in her own way."

"You don't know what she's capable of."

That brought me up short. "Tallulah, what are you saying? You don't think your mother murdered Hugh, do you?"

The color drained from her face. "No, no, no, no, no." She shook her head violently.

"Then what are you worried about?"

"I can't tell you. You, more than anyone, I can't tell." She turned and fled the room.

"Tallulah!" I chased her across the hall into the ladies room. "Tallulah!" She rushed into a stall and threw the lock. "Tallulah, come out. What's the matter? What did your mom—?"

The door to the ladies room swung open and

two women walked in chatting about a third woman. I went to the sink and rinsed my hands. "I have to go," I called out casually. "Will you make my excuses to the family?"

"Where shall I say you went?" Tallulah's relieved voice echoed from the stall.

"Tell them I needed air."

On the street, I pressed call, waiting impatiently for Chris. I wanted to meet with Detective Salinsky as soon as possible, but the repeated pattern of Chris's calls intrigued me. Maybe he wanted to apologize—to say his statement about spending winters in the Keys had been a momentary lapse, not meant to be taken seriously. When he answered, I heard music and chatter in the background. "Julia. Hang on a minute. I'm in a bar. I'll step outside."

In a bar? I erased the image of regret my imagination had etched on his handsome face. "You tried to reach me?" I sounded like a harried executive barking at a subordinate. I cleared my throat and tried for a softer, more girlfriend-like tone. "Sorry. I had my phone off at the memorial reception."

He didn't seem to notice my bark. "I got a flight out."

This was news? I hadn't realized he didn't have one. "That's good. Tell me when and I'll meet you."

"I get into Logan at three-thirty tomorrow."

"Tomorrow? I thought you were due back on Saturday."

"I didn't want to take the chance. What did you think I meant when I said I got a flight? With the storm coming, the airlines are crazy."

Storm coming? What kind of storms did they have in Key West in February? "Is it a hurricane?"

There was a burst of noise and laughter behind him. "What? I can't hear you! I'm moving down the street."

"Is it a hurricane?" I repeated.

"A hurricane? Of course not. It's a nor'easter and it's headed in your direction. They're talking three feet of snow in two separate storms. The airline said if I didn't fly home tomorrow it might be into next week. Have you been living in a bubble?"

Evidently. "When is this coming?"

"Starts up there tonight, but that will be the least of it. There'll be a break tomorrow—that's when I hope to get in—and then it'll start up again late afternoon."

"Maine too?" I could imagine Sonny's furious preparations.

"Maine too. I think you should pick me up at the airport and we'll head straight home."

I didn't respond. Things were so unsettled here, but suddenly, I wanted nothing more than to be home, in my little town, in my little apartment, going through my little routine. With Chris.

"Julia? Did you hear me?"

"Yes, yes. I'll meet you at the airport tomorrow with your truck."

Another burst of random yelling, more like roaring, traveled through the phone. "Good. See you then. Love you."

"Love you too. Bye."

Chapter 27

I walked quickly, head down, wishing I had more practical footwear than the pumps I'd worn to the memorial. My phone told me the police station was a mile and a half away. The temperature had dropped while I'd been inside the Harvard Club. The wind slapped my cheeks, bringing tears to my eyes. I looked along Mass. Ave. for a cab, but none appeared, unsurprising given the weather and the time of day. Uber told me my best-case ride was ten minutes out and expensive. I kept walking.

The Area Five building was surrounded by squad cars and other police vehicles. Uniformed cops bustled in and out of the building, bundled up in long, waterproof overcoats and caps. The scene in the reception area was equally busy. I fought my way to the front desk and asked for Detective Salinsky.

He appeared right away and escorted me to

a conference room. We sat across from one another. He pulled a pen and his small notebook from the pocket of his sports jacket.

"You needed to see me urgently," he said.

As if I needed reminding. "I've been at Hugh Morales's memorial reception, where I met a woman named Hoover. She employed Paolo Paolini before Hugh and Marguerite did. Then I met a couple named Jenkins and a woman named Price, who had employed Paolo prior to that. They each told me an interesting story." I recounted their histories as I understood them. Three terminally ill patients. Three quiet, peaceful deaths, each one after the family had gathered and said good-bye. Each one expected, yet surprising in its own way. Each one unattended, in a house filled with family.

When I was done, Salinsky put his pen down. I noticed he hadn't written anything, not even the names of Paolo's former employers. "The people you spoke to didn't mention any doubts?"

"The deaths were expected. Both Claire Hoover and Mrs. Price expressed some regret that their family member was alone at the time of their passing, but no suspicion. These deaths were largely a relief to the family, and to the person who died."

He furrowed his bushy eyebrows. "You're telling me about a 'killer angel' type who takes matters into his own hands when he believes his patients have suffered enough. I can see how you reached this conclusion. Taken together, these cases look worrisome. We never would have looked into Hugh Morales's death if someone hadn't called to express suspicion."

He sat back in his chair. "I checked you out, you know. Lieutenant Jerry Binder of the Maine State Police speaks of you highly, says you've got tremendous instincts. Unfortunately, you are wrong in this case. Mr. Paolini is not a suspect in Hugh Morales's death."

"Even after what I've told you? Why not?"

"Because it was Mr. Paolini who called us and tipped us off. We never would have begun this investigation if it weren't for Mr. Paolini." Salinsky's thick lips turned up into something that came up short of a smile.

My cheeks felt hot with embarrassment and disappointment. I'd been sure I was onto something with Paolo.

"Is that all you've come to tell me?" Salinsky asked.

I grasped at straws. "What about Clive? Have you looked into him?"

Salinsky nodded. "Yup. He's no more Clive Humphries than I'm the queen of England." He paused. "Though it's not, strictly speaking, illegal, to go by a name other than your own."

"Even if you marry under false pretenses? He and Vivian got married yesterday."

The eyebrows rose. "Seems like odd timing."

"Doesn't it? Is it true wives can't be compelled to testify against their husbands?"

"Depends on the circumstances, but yes, that is generally true. Has Mr. Humphries done anything to incriminate himself since I saw you yesterday?"

I hesitated. I'd already made one wrong accusation today. I thought about the dramatic dinner the night before and my conversation with Clive on the front stoop that morning. Really, there was nothing new. "Do you think Clive murdered Hugh?" I asked.

"I'm not prepared to discuss that with you. But tell me, what's his motive?"

"The town house. It's got to be worth a fortune, and now that he's married to Vivian . . ." I let the thought hang out there.

Salinksy steepled his sausagelike fingers. "Hugh owned the town house in joint tenancy with Marguerite Morales. Dr. Morrow assures me Mrs. Morales could live several more years. If Clive was moving Hugh out of the way to speed up the timeline for Vivian to inherit, all he had to do was wait. It's Mrs. Morales who's the obstacle, not Hugh. I go back to the question I've asked from the beginning. Who benefited from Hugh dying a few days early?"

Salinsky walked me back to the reception area, which still bustled with uniformed officers. He gestured toward the crowd. "We're getting ready for the storm tonight. Never am I as happy to be out of uniform as I am during a blizzard. There will be traffic accidents, power outages that take out traffic lights and trap people in elevators, heart attacks where the ambulances can't get down the road. The busier the uniforms are, the less busy I am. You can't do a drive-by when you literally can't drive by."

"I'm supposed to go back to Maine tomorrow."

Salinsky looked out the big windows at the low, gray sky. "Then you'd better get out early, before the second part of this storm comes through. I hear it's going to be a doozy."

Chapter 28

I arrived back at the town house at the same time as the group returning from the memorial. Jake and Paolo held on to Marguerite as she made her way across the sidewalk to the house.

She put a hand out to me. "I'm going inside to rest. You and Rose will be my guests at my favorite restaurant tonight. I've told the others they're on their own. I would like to spend some time with my out-of-town guests. The car will pick us up at seven."

Everyone scattered. The house was quiet, except for the sound of Tallulah's throaty voice, accompanied by Jake on the piano. She sang a bluesy tune I didn't recognize. The lovely, sad sound floated through the house.

I hovered close to the pocket doors to the living room. Especially after striking out with my Paolo theory, I wanted to talk to Tallulah about our conversation in the coatroom. What had she meant about her mother? But she and Jake continued rehearsing with no sign of a break. I went to my room.

There was a knock on the door. "Come in."

Paolo entered, his expression grave, his big, sad eyes somehow bigger and sadder. "We must talk," he said. His voice was low and serious. "Today at the reception, you thought I had killed Mr. Hugh." I had to strain to hear him. The only place to sit in the sparsely furnished room was on my bed. We huddled awkwardly, side by side.

"I did," I admitted.

"But I was the one who called the police."

"I know. I spoke to Detective Salinsky." I shifted on the bed to face him. "Paolo, I'm sorry for what I suspected. I heard the same story three times—four if you count Hugh—someone terminally ill who holds on until their family arrives to say good-bye, and then that night, drifts away in their sleep while no one is there. It seemed like more than a coincidence."

"It is more than a coincidence, Ms. Julia. It is my job. After everything is settled, and all the words have been spoken, and everyone is gone, I tell my patients, 'You can let go now.' Then I leave them alone, so they have no obligation to me or to anyone else, and they go." He spoke confidently, like someone who was good at his work, and knew it. "You would be amazed how many people, old, sick, in pain, exhausted, stay here just to be polite to us, the healthy and the living. All I do is give them permission."

"But how did you know Hugh hadn't drifted off? Why did you suspect he was killed?"

"Because he wasn't ready. I hadn't given him this permission."

"Rose was here. He'd said his good-byes."

Paolo trained his eyes on me. "He had one thing left to do. One major wrong he needed to make right. He needed to reach out to your mother."

Chapter 29

The town car idled by the curb, double-parked and snarling late rush hour traffic. I helped Rose bring Marguerite down the front steps. I had to admire her. At ninety-six, I thought I would have chosen to stay in on a February night when snow was predicted. She was light as a bird, which came in handy again when we got to the curb and had to lift her over the snow bank. I was worried all the handling might hurt her, but she showed her surprising strength and didn't protest.

When we were settled in the limo, we glided off into the night. I didn't know where we were headed. The city was a tangle of stoplights, one-way streets, and aggressive driving performed in small spaces. There were plenty of delightful-looking restaurants right in Marguerite's neighborhood. I had trouble understanding why we had to leave it.

The car brought us at last over a bridge and

then swept into a parking lot bordered by modern brick buildings. The driver stopped at the last building and we got out. "That's the federal courthouse," Marguerite said, pointing to the next building over. "All the big trials are there. Whitey Bulger, the Boston Marathon bomber. I come down to watch them when I have a chance."

Over the top of Marguerite's head, Rose raised an eyebrow at me. This was a new side of our elderly cousin. We walked through the archway at the end of the row of buildings and the silhouette of the city opened up in front of us. In the foreground was the harbor, and then the city lights behind it—the new skyscrapers and hotels, and the old Custom House.

"You should see this on a summer night." Marguerite's arm swept the plaza area. "The restaurant has seating out here and it is delightful. The thought of a summer evening at the Daily Catch makes me want to stay on this earth for one more ride around the sun." She took both our arms, folding them in hers. "Thank you for coming out with me and reminding me how wonderful life can be. It's been hard to contemplate going on since Hugh died."

We stepped inside the restaurant, which was as intimate and warm as the plaza was sweeping. A smiling woman rushed over to us. "Mrs. Morales, how lovely to see you again. Your regular table is ready."

"Thank you." Marguerite led the way to a corner table. When we were seated she ordered a Manhattan and urged Rose and me to try one. I was skeptical, but Marguerite was a hard woman to say no to. I nodded my head and the waiter strode away.

"I have brought you both here," Marguerite said, "because the Daily Catch has the very best fish in Boston. Julia, you know something about the preparation of fish, and being from San Francisco, Rose, I suspect you do too."

Rose squinted at the menu. "It looks wonderful."

'That's something that has stayed in the genes," Marguerite said. "We are all in different cities, living different lives, but we all live near the sea."

We chatted until the waiter returned and we made our selections, monkfish marsala over pasta for Marguerite—"my usual"—while Rose and I fell to the temptation of a calamari salad followed by lobster fra diavolo, all signature dishes at the Daily Catch. Marguerite added a bottle of Montepulciano to the order. She kept up a pleasant commentary about the memorial and the guests. As we drank our Manhattans, Rose and I followed along, asking about this person and that, even though there were so many other things I was dying to talk about.

The waiter arrived with our appetizers. The calamari was like none I had ever tasted. Its texture paired beautifully with the crunch of the salad greens and vegetables. Beneath the vinegary, lemony flavors of the dressing, the squid retained a hint of its origins in the ocean.

When I looked up from my salad, both my tablemates were staring at me. Rose gave a slight nod of her head, and Marguerite spoke.

"Julia, I'm afraid we've brought you here under false pretenses. You still haven't told us why you came to Boston. If Mr. Dickison didn't contact you, how did you find us? We hoped, if it was just Rose and me, apart from the others, you would tell us the truth."

Cuthie Cuthbertson had counseled caution and Detective Salinsky had asked me outright not to talk about the Black Widow. Yet, these women had been so kind to me. They had taken me into their hearts and now Marguerite had taken me quite literally into her home. I wanted to repay their straightforwardness with my own. The Manhattan followed by the Montepulciano gave me courage. "Someone sent a valuable necklace to my mother days before Hugh died. A black diamond with twenty-four white diamonds. I came to Boston to find out who sent it."

"The Black Widow!" Marguerite's eyes danced. "It's been missing for almost a hundred years."

"What's the Black Widow?" Rose asked.

"It's a necklace that belonged to our family. The main stone is a black diamond, seventy carats."

Rose's fork clattered onto her appetizer plate. "That's crazy."

"I think Hugh had it all along," I told them.

"He couldn't have had it all along," Marguerite pointed out. "The necklace went missing in 1928."

I turned to Rose, who'd picked up her fork and dug back into her calamari. "Could he have taken it from your grandparents' house when he helped you clean it out?" I asked.

"I suppose." She sounded unsure. "He never said anything, and he took so little. Trinkets, really."

"The Black Widow is in an inventory of his personal property that Mr. Dickison has," I added. "So Hugh thought it was his to leave to someone."

"Then he meant it to go to your mother." Marguerite stated it as a fact.

"It came with a note that said, 'For Windsholme,' and the package was mailed before Hugh died," I told them.

"Someone in the house mailed it," Marguerite concluded. "And your mother is meant to use the money to repair Windsholme."

"Yes, I think so too, though everything else about the necklace is a mystery. Who sent it and why they sent it instead of leaving it to be distributed as part of the estate."

Marguerite studied her silverware and said in a low voice, "Whoever sent it didn't trust that it would get to your mother safely after Hugh was gone."

I could understand her embarrassment. She was casting suspicion on her own family.

"I don't understand how Hugh could have been the legal owner of the Black Widow," I said. "If it was stolen by Hugh's grandparents from your mother, Marguerite, then it must be yours. Or, if it legitimately belonged to Hugh's family, then it should have been in his parents' estate. He was officially dead and couldn't inherit when they died, so it would be yours, Rose."

There was silence around the table while the waiter cleared the salad dishes and served our entrees. Marguerite dug into her monkfish marsala with gusto. "You girls are in for a treat." After she's finished her first mouthful, she said, "I can clear some of this up. There was a dispute about the ownership of the necklace. Your great-great-grandfathers, William and Charles, believed the necklace was a gift from Lemuel Morrow to their mother, Sarah, and as such should have been a part of her small estate, which was left to them when she died in 1906. They said their father had no right to give the necklace to my mother in the first place. My mother firmly believed the necklace belonged to her, a gift from her husband during their loving but tragically short marriage.

"When there was plenty of money around, my half brothers were content to let my mother keep possession of the necklace and wear it, though they always saw her as a temporary custodian, with the necklace coming to them or their heirs on her death. But by 1928, all three families were desperately short of cash and the arguments grew angrier. Lemuel had left the ice business and Morrow Island to his sons. My mother got only the house on Marlborough Street and some money to run it. Most of the money was in the form of shares in Morrow

Ice Company, which were worthless by then. William had no money and was likely to lose Morrow Island because of unpaid property taxes. Charles's family had not yet hit it big in San Francisco.

"The night the necklace disappeared, Windsholme was full of guests, every room occupied. It was Prohibition, but the booze flowed. My mother still maintained her role as hostess at Windsholme, even though the house belonged to her stepsons, and she knew how to give a good party. The next morning, I heard my mother scream. When I reached her room, she was in hysterics, holding up the empty jewelry case.

"The rumors started that day. Some people said it was a maid who took it. Other people blamed a houseguest. William, Charles, and my mother, Clementine, blamed each other. They all needed cash, and the necklace, while beautiful, didn't provide any. After the houseguests left there was a terrific, multigenerational row with everyone screaming accusations at everyone else. Things were said that couldn't be unsaid. The relationships, always tense after William lost the ice company's money, became irreparable. Charles's family packed up and left that day. Mother and I left early the next morning."

"And they never resolved who owned the Black Widow, your mother or your half brothers?" I asked.

"There was no need. The necklace was gone."

Marguerite looked off into the middle distance of the restaurant, which was nearly empty. "I would so love to see it again."

Rose spoke quietly. "Someone in my branch of the family, Charles or his son, must have stolen the Black Widow. Over the next decade, my ancestors built a fortune in shipping. My grandfather told me the family bought ships when others sold them cheap during the Depression. They built up a huge fleet. They must have used the Black Widow as collateral over and over. Otherwise, how could they have bought that first ship and expanded so quickly?"

"Shipping," Marguerite said, "was the engine of the ice business. Charles returned to something he knew."

"Then, your grandparents must have had the Black Widow and Hugh must have taken it," I said to Rose.

"If Hugh left it to your mother, she should have it," Rose said to me. Marguerite nodded her agreement.

"It's worth over two million dollars," I told them.

Rose said, "Wow."

"Well, it would be, wouldn't it," Marguerite responded.

The table fell silent as we concentrated on our meals. I tried to think through the problem of the ownership of the Black Widow. No one knew whom it belonged to then or now, exactly the mess Cuthie Cuthbertson had predicted.

The lobster fra diavolo grabbed my attention,

pulling me back into the moment. I consider myself something of an expert on lobster, and the fra diavolo at the Daily Catch was the best I'd ever tasted. It was served in a sauté pan, the pieces of lobster, shrimp, clams, and calamari gently distributed over a bed of pasta. The sauce had a velvety consistency that absorbed the savory taste of seafood. The shellfish was perfectly cooked, tender and briny. The heat, the "diavolo" came at the end, adding a pleasant warmth, but not overpowering the flavors.

"Have some monkfish." Marguerite put a piece of flaky white fish on her bread plate and passed it over. I admit I was skeptical. Marsala was a sweet wine, and I thought it would overwhelm the light fish, but the combination was delightful. Each flavor enhanced the other.

"It's wonderful," I said.

"Now you understand why this is my favorite restaurant."

"Why is the necklace called the Black Widow?" Rose asked. So, she too had been unable to get the necklace out of her head, despite the delicious seafood.

"It wasn't, originally." Marguerite chuckled. "My mother was of French descent, from Louisiana. Her father had been a local partner in the Morrow icehouse there. She was the belle of high society in New Orleans, but when Lemuel brought her to Boston, her olive skin and her Catholicism made her exotic. She was forty years younger than my father. Her origins plus the tremendous age difference made their marriage scandalous. He died less than eighteen months after they married, before I was born. The rumor was that she'd 'worn him out,' though I didn't understand what that meant until I was much older. She was called the Black Widow behind her back. She wore the necklace so often, eventually it was referred to as the Black Widow as well. After it disappeared, the name stuck to the necklace. Everyone called it that."

The waiter came and cleared our plates. "Dessert?" he asked.

Marguerite didn't hesitate. "The usual, and three forks." Rose and I ordered espressos.

The usual turned out to be a lemon mascarpone cake so creamy, tart, and sweet, I was disappointed I hadn't ordered my own piece, even though I was stuffed from the lobster and pasta.

"Do you really intend to leave your house to Tallulah?" Rose asked Marguerite.

Marguerite sighed. "No, probably not. Tallulah is fiercely loyal and would feel she had to keep it. A big house like that, in need of constant maintenance, is more of a curse than a blessing for a young person. I want Tallulah and Jake to tour the world with their act. I don't want her anchored by an albatross of a piece of property."

I nodded my agreement. At times, Windsholme felt like an albatross to me.

"Vivian loves the house and really seems to want it," Rose chided softly.

"I know," Marguerite admitted. "But I'm determined Clive won't get it. Or any future Clive.

I think some sort of a trust should do the trick. It should be in a trust for tax reasons now that Hugh's dead. I'll call Adam Dickison tomorrow to talk over options."

The town car driver walked into the restaurant, snow on his shoulders and cap. "It's really comin' down," he said. "There's a snow emuhgency in effect at midnight. Everybody off the roads. The city wants to get 'em cleared before the second stawm comes in tahmahra."

I looked around the restaurant. We were the only table still occupied. The waiter and hostess sat in a far booth folding napkins while they waited for us to finish. Outside the big windows, the streetlights along the harbor walk reflected swirls of big-flaked snow, like the angels were having a pillow fight.

"Time to go!" Marguerite chirped, and whipped out her credit card.

Chapter 30

The espresso turned out to be a bad idea. I lay in the unfamiliar bed, unable to sleep. Paolo's door opened and soft footsteps moved toward the bathroom. I waited, wakeful, until I heard him go back to his room. The pattern was repeated on the second floor. Someone was up, but that person, too, returned to a bedroom. I heard the click of a door. From outside, the wind shook the windows, quieted down, but then whipped up again into great gusts. I got up and looked out into the side street. The snow flew sideways from the river. Looking carefully, I could discern a single lane plowed in the street below, but even it was rapidly filling in with drifting snow.

The old iron radiator creaked and sighed in the corner of the room. So much had happened. It was strange to think it was my first night in the house Lemuel Morrow had bought for Sarah, and where he'd lived as a widower, and later with

Clementine. None of my ancestors, surely, had slept in this little attic room, where the mansard roof created odd angles in the walls. I listened to the sounds of a strange house and wondered if I would sleep at all. Eventually I dozed.

A scream. Someone in my dream screamed and wouldn't stop. But it wasn't a dream. I heard footsteps pounding down the stairs, running in the hallway.

"Help, help! She's not breathing!" Tallulah shouted. Paolo had run down the stairs ahead of me. Rose was already in Marguerite's room, breathing into her mouth and rhythmically compressing her chest. Marguerite was prone on the floor, so tiny and so thin, I flinched with each chest compression. Tallulah and Vivian clung to each other, faces twisted in terror.

"Paolo, help me with her. Someone else call nine-one-one," Rose commanded.

"I'll do it," Jake said.

"Go down, turn on the front porch light, make sure the EMTs can find us," Rose continued.

"Got it." I ran downstairs, jumped into my boots, and pulled my down coat over my T-shirt and pajama pants.

"The ambulance is on its way," Jake called, "but the roads are bad. They're keeping me on the line until they get here."

Despite the wind, the front stoop had more than a foot of snow on it, and Marlborough Street held even more. I didn't see how an ambulance could get down it. I found a shovel in the front vestibule and went to work knocking

snow off the stoop into the little garden below
and then started on the steps. The falling snow
piled up on the back of my coat and wicked
down my neck.

I had shoveled half the length of the walk
when at last I saw flashing lights, coming not
down Marlborough Street, but down the side
street, Dartmouth. The first yellow lights belonged to a slow-moving plow, followed by the
blue lights of a Boston Police Department cruiser,
the red lights of a fire truck, followed at last by
an ambulance. They slowed to a stop, idling in
the road.

A police officer was the first to reach the walk.
The snow on the unshoveled part was above his
knees. By the time I let him in and directed him
up the stairs, there were people in heavy outerwear everywhere, carrying big bags and running up the front steps. When they were all
inside, I stepped into the hall. From upstairs, I
could hear Rose give the EMTs a calm recital of
Marguerite's condition and what had been
done so far.

I went back outside. Some of the firemen
shoveled a path between the curb and the ambulance. The plow moved snow out of the intersection so the vehicles could turn around. I
bounced up and down in my boots, anxious to
help but determined to stay out of the way.

The cop came outside. "They're taking her to
Mass General."

She must be alive! A tear welled over my eye
and slid down my frozen cheek. I had known

Marguerite only three days, but she was already dear to me.

Four men carried the gurney to the ambulance. There was no way to wheel it. Rose stayed by Marguerite's side, holding her motionless hand. She was waxen and still, and so, so small. I ran after Rose. "At the hospital, you need to have them test her for drugs that might have caused this."

"I've got her medications with me." Rose didn't stop to look at me. All her attention was on Marguerite. "Vivian got them for me from the medicine chest."

"No, that's not what I mean. You need to make sure she wasn't poisoned."

Rose stopped and turned while the EMTs loaded the gurney into the ambulance. "What are you talking about?"

"Last night, I had an attack when I couldn't breathe. I've had panic attacks before, so I didn't say anything, but now, I think maybe it was caused by a poison of some sort."

One of the EMTs shouted something that was carried away by the wind, but the urgency was obvious. "I've got to go," Rose shouted. "Call Detective Salinsky. Have him meet me at the hospital." She turned and ran along the snow-covered street.

I ran beside her, yelling in her ear. "Have them check for feathers and fibers in her throat too."

She nodded at me and was gone.

They let Rose ride in the back. She was a

doctor, after all. And then, more quickly than I dreamed possible, they were gone—the plow, the ambulance, the cop car. The fire engine turned laboriously to go back the way it had come, the wrong way down the street. Though their sirens wailed, the vehicles left at a creep.

Just inside the threshold, Vivian and Tallulah clung to each other, weeping, barefoot, and in their nightclothes, all animosity between them evaporated by their fear.

Chapter 31

Tallulah, Jake, and I decided to hike to the hospital. After we'd dressed and bundled up, we stood on the front stoop and surveyed the street. The snow was still coming down, though it had lightened. The cars parked along a single side of the street were covered. From the look of the quiet, night-time landscape, it could have been 1888 when Lemuel moved Sarah into the house, or 1919 when Clementine arrived, or anytime in the last hundred and thirty years.

"Let's walk around to Beacon Street," Jake said. "It's more likely to be plowed."

We trudged down the middle of Beacon Street to the end and then around the corner of the public garden to Charles Street. The wind had stopped. The city was silent. It was only a little over a mile from Marguerite's house to Mass General, less than I'd walked to the police station that afternoon, but even staying in the partially plowed roads, the snow made for slow going. It took three-quarters of an hour to reach the emergency room door at Mass General.

The receptionist couldn't give us much in the way of an update. We huddled in the quiet waiting room. The snow had kept the city's emergencies in check, just as Detective Salinsky had predicted. The sun came up, shadowy at first, but then lighting up a dazzling blue sky, the calm between the storms. A new shift came in. They stomped snow off their boots and complained about the travel conditions.

"How did you find your grandmother?" I asked Tallulah.

"When I got up to go to the bathroom, her door was open, which was strange. I went to check it out and found her lying on the bedroom floor, like she was trying to get out the door when she collapsed."

"Thank goodness you found her, Lulah," Jake said.

"Yes," I agreed. "Thank goodness."

Rose emerged from the back a few minutes later. "She's still unconscious. I broke two of her ribs doing the compressions, but she's come through. Nothing to do now but wait. They'll move her upstairs once they're confident she's stable."

"Can we see her?" Tallulah asked.

"Soon, but you mustn't expect a response for a while."

Tallulah grimaced. "I just want to see her."

"Do you need coffee?" Rose pulled on my

arm, steering me toward the vending machines at the other side of the room. When we were there, she bent her head toward mine and whispered, "Salinsky's here. He wants to see you. It looks like you were right."

"She was poisoned?"

"They don't have the lab work yet to confirm it, but the way she's coming out of this, it's not like a physical episode, more like some substance is working its way through her system. No sign of feathers or fibers, by the way."

"When I thought about it later, I didn't think there would be. Marguerite is so small, if someone wanted to smother her, they would have succeeded."

They let Tallulah see her grandmother at a little before eight. Jake went with her, saying he'd wait nearby in case he was needed. I knew he meant needed by Tallulah, not Marguerite. Tallulah had much better taste in men than her mother did.

"You were right."

I jumped, turning around as I did.

Detective Salinksy stood behind me in the waiting room. "Rose told me you were the one who realized Mrs. Morales needed to be tested. Beta-blockers, it looks like. She was poisoned with an overdose of her own medication. Enough to kill her if her granddaughter hadn't found her, and if she hadn't had a doctor and a hospice nurse staying at her house. Especially

with the delay of the EMTs due to the storm."
He inclined his head toward the hallway. "Let's
talk."

He led me to a cafeteria on the ground floor
of another building on the dense MGH campus.
Around us tables full of medical personnel
talked and joked as coworkers do, while families
and friends of the patients quietly played with
their meals. A man with a toddler and a pre-
schooler attempted to load food on a tray while
the younger one, a little girl, screamed to be
picked up. He turned to Salinsky and me. "I'm
sorry about the noise. I had to bring them
today. Their mom . . ." His eyes welled and the
tray wobbled.

"Not a problem," Salinsky said, grabbing the
tray. "I had two close in age like that myself."
Salinsky carried the tray to the cashier while the
man picked up the little girl and took his son's
hand. Salinsky paid for the food, along with our
coffees.

"I can't let you do that," the man protested,
and tried to fish his wallet out of his back pocket.

"On me," Salinsky said in a tone that left the
man no choice.

After the overburdened father thanked us for
the third time, Salinsky and I found a table in a
corner of the cavernous room. The babble around
us created a zone for private conversation.

"Until she wakes up and tells me she took
those pills on purpose or accidentally, I'm treat-
ing this as an attempt on Mrs. Morales's life,"
Salinksy said.

"I don't believe she took them on purpose," I said. "She was sad about Hugh's death, but not despondent. We had a wonderful dinner last night. She was engaged, telling stories. She told Rose and me she wanted to live for at least one more trip around the sun."

"That's what Dr. Morrow told me as well. I don't imagine you get to Mrs. Morales's age without developing skills for coping with the passing of people you care about. She's ninety-six. She's not ill, but she can't live forever. Who benefits from her dying sooner than later?"

"Isn't that the same question you asked about Hugh?"

Salinsky took a sip of his coffee. It was black and steam rose off it. He winced slightly when the liquid hit his tongue. "It is, though in his case, the question is who benefited from him dying days before he would have otherwise. In Mrs. Morales's case, Dr. Morrow says it could be years. She also told me the reason you thought Mrs. Morales should be tested was because you believed there had been an attempt on your life."

I blushed. "I didn't think so at the time. I'm prone to panic attacks, though it didn't seem like a panic attack to me. When I saw Marguerite struggling to breathe, I wondered. That's why I said what I did to Rose."

Salinsky drained his coffee cup. "Why would someone want to kill you?"

I'd wondered that since I'd first said the words to Rose. "I don't think anyone did try to kill me.

After a tense family dinner the night before last, Marguerite, Rose, and I went into the living room for after-dinner drinks. There were brandies on a tray, already poured. I think Marguerite was meant to take the glass closest to her chair, but instead, Rose picked up the tray the glasses were on and offered Marguerite a different one."

"You got the glass intended for Marguerite."

I pictured Rose's graceful motion as she had picked up the tray, turning it toward Marguerite and then offering a drink to me. "Yes, I think that's what happened."

"You said this was after a tense family meal. What caused the tension?"

"Clive and Vivian had married that afternoon. Clive acted quite proprietarily toward the town house. He talked about the changes he and Vivian would make when Marguerite was dead. Marguerite told them they would never get the house. She'd leave it to Tallulah."

Salinsky's expression didn't change. I imagined it took a lot to shock him. "Who poured these brandies?"

"Rose thought Paolo had done it while she and I were clearing the table, but in reality, anyone in the house could have. I only got sick, a feeling of fatigue I couldn't shake, difficulty breathing. I didn't pass out like Marguerite did, but I'm younger and bigger."

"Our perpetrator may not know what he's doing in any precise way. He could be guessing at dosages." Salinsky paused. "There's no point in testing you now. These drugs run through your system in six hours. The rapidity of Mrs. Morales's recovery is one of the indicators of what happened to her. So, you think our erstwhile Mr. Clive Humphries poisoned Marguerite to get control of the house?"

"Marguerite told Rose and me last night she planned to speak with Mr. Dickison today about moving the property into a trust."

"Interesting timing, at a minimum. The amount of beta-blockers in Mrs. Morales's body should be enough for us to get a warrant to search the house."

"Be sure to check the glass on her bedside table. She always kept water there. She told Rose and me she drank a glassful whenever she'd had alcohol. She had a cocktail last night and we split a bottle of wine."

"We'll check it, if it's still there. And we'll interview everyone at the house, except 'Mr. Humphries,' whom we'll take to the station for his questioning. I'd like to have him as on edge as possible."

"I plan to go home to Maine this afternoon," I reminded him.

"No reason you shouldn't. I have your contact information. I'll find you when I need you."

Salinsky shifted in his chair. "There's one thing that bothers me. Marguerite was given an overdose of beta-blockers, you think in a drink. You may have ingested beta-blockers too, also in a drink. But Hugh Morales was smothered. Why?"

"Was he too weak to drink, perhaps?"

"Not that anyone has told me. I interviewed both Mr. Paolini and Mr. Morales's physician extensively about his physical condition. The patient was in pain. He hadn't left that room in a month. He was eating little, but still taking liquids by mouth." He paused. "Besides, it doesn't make sense that Humphries would murder him. He had only days to wait for Morales to die naturally. I come back, every time, to the question of who benefited from the timing of Hugh Morales's death."

Chapter 32

Marguerite had been assigned a room. Rose texted me the number. I followed the signs, got turned around twice, and had to ask for directions. While I walked, my phone buzzed with a text. **In Charlotte. Boarding. Looks like I got lucky. Love.** I heaved a sigh of relief. Chris had made it out between storms. In three hours I'd pick him up and we'd be on the way home.

On the right path at last, I entered an elevator and punched the button for the top floor. When the doors opened, I exited into a lounge area that wouldn't have looked out of place at the Harvard Club. The woodwork was mahogany, the furniture antique. I found Tallulah asleep on a guest bed in Marguerite's room. Marguerite appeared to sleep too, though I wasn't sure that was the right word for it. Her eyeballs moved restlessly behind her thin lids. Her hands fluttered and her leg occasionally kicked at the bedclothes. I hated seeing her like that. She was old, but she'd been so alive. I took her hand and squeezed it lightly. "We'll have dinner again at the Daily Catch this summer," I promised. "We'll sit outside and watch the sun go down."

The room looked more like it was in a fancy hotel than a hospital, except for the bed, the monitor, and the IV drip hooked up to Marguerite. I went to the big window and looked out. The view swept down the Charles. It was panoramic in the daytime and would be spectacular at night.

A uniformed policeman stood outside the room. Rose appeared in the doorway. "Detective Salinsky sent him," she said, with a flick of her head, indicating the officer.

"Won't he attract attention?"

"At Phillips House?" Rose smiled. "She's probably the only one who checked in without a bodyguard. This is where the rich and famous come to get their ills cured. The rich, the famous, and little old ladies of a certain Boston class, like Marguerite."

"She must have the best Medicare supplemental insurance in the world."

Rose laughed. "I may have pulled a few strings. Professional courtesy."

"Is she all right?"

"She will be. She's had a major assault on her system, both from the drug overdose and from those of us who worked to save her. It will take a while for her to come out of it, but there are no signs of permanent damage."

"Salinsky and others will be at the town house soon," I told her. "They'll search for whatever did this to Marguerite. They'll interview most of the family there, but Clive they'll take to the station."

She nodded to show she understood. "Jake and I are headed back to the house to get cleaned up and maybe rest. Tallulah will stay. I'll be back in time to see the doctor when he comes this afternoon."

"I'll stay too."

"I thought you had to pick up your boyfriend at the airport."

"I have some time."

I stayed for an hour and a half. Marguerite slumbered on, though she had some color in her face and her rest seemed less troubled.

Tallulah woke up and stretched. "How long was I asleep?" Her gaze flew to her grandmother. "How is she?"

"Better, I think. Rose seems pretty confident."

"Thank God."

I gestured toward the corridor. "We need to talk." We walked into the hallway where Tallulah spotted the uniformed officer and recoiled. I pulled her along to the empty, elegant patient lounge. We were the only ones there.

"Tallulah, what did you mean yesterday in the coatroom, when you told me I didn't know what your mother was capable of?"

Tallulah perched on a couch with an ornate,

carved back. She shook her head and kept her lips sealed.

"Do you think your mother is capable of killing your grandmother, or Hugh?" I'd asked her before and she'd denied it, but after what had happened to Marguerite, perhaps Tallulah had second thoughts.

She didn't. "No! Mummy loves Granny. And she loved Hugh. She would *never . . .*"

"You heard your grandmother threaten to leave the town house directly to you. That's millions of dollars of motive."

Tallulah shook her head. "That's the way the two of them are all the time. Granny always threatens, but she never goes through with it."

"The threat didn't mean much until Hugh died," I reminded her.

She hesitated for a second. I could tell she was considering the implications. Then she repeated, "No, Mummy would never."

"Then what did you mean yesterday in the coatroom?" I pressed. "What is your mother capable of?"

"I . . . she . . . it's just that . . ." She took a deep breath. "I think my mother stole something really valuable that Hugh meant to leave to your mother."

"A necklace with a big, black diamond?"

"Yes! How did you know?"

"It's in a safety deposit box in Busman's Harbor, Maine."

"Why? How? Omigosh, I am so relieved."

"It came in the US mail, addressed to my mom,"

I told her. "Uninsured. No return address. How long have you known about it?"

"The necklace? All my life. When I was little, Hugh used to let me play princess with it, but only in his room. He asked me not to tell anyone about it. He told me it had been his mother's."

"But you did. Tell someone, that is."

She hung her head. "I told my mother. I didn't think anything of it. I never believed the gems were real. Then I got too old for dress-up and I almost, sort of, forgot about it."

"Until?"

"Until one night at dinner, about two weeks before Hugh died. It was just me, Granny, and Mummy. Clive was out. It was Paolo's night off and Jake was sitting upstairs with Hugh. Anyway, sort of out of the blue, Granny brings up this famous necklace that had belonged to her mother. The Black Widow, she called it. I looked at Mummy and Mummy looked at me, and we knew. Mr. Dickison had come to the house a few months before, and Hugh told us he'd changed his will to leave his personal effects to Jacqueline. 'A bunch of old junk,' my mother had said at the time, but once Granny talked about the necklace, we both knew different.

"The next day, I went to read to Hugh, and he fell asleep. I looked in his top drawer. That's where the necklace should have been. It was gone. I searched the whole room. Later, when Mom and Clive went out, I looked in her room. I found it right away, in the toe of one of her shoes. She hadn't even tried hard to hide it. Did she think I'd just go along?

"I brought it back and told Hugh what had happened. He said, 'Don't worry. I'll take care of it.' We were so distracted after that. Hugh was obviously going to die soon. I didn't forget about the necklace, but it wasn't the most important thing to me, either. After Hugh died, I checked and it was gone again. I was sure my mother took it." Tallulah smiled for the first time that day. "But it's okay. Your mom has it. Hugh did take care of it."

"Yes, he did." I gave her a hug. "That's one thing you don't have to worry about."

She returned my embrace. "I don't have to, but you do. Mummy's never going to let you keep it without a fight."

Chapter 33

I returned to Marguerite's house the way we'd come the night before. On Charles Street, the sidewalks were plowed and the coffee shops and restaurants open. Traffic was light. The governor had asked everyone who could to stay home, and many had complied. As I walked, I turned Detective Salinsky's question over in my mind. "Who benefited by Hugh dying a few days sooner?"

When I arrived at the door of the town house, Vivian had her coat on. "That Detective Salinsky was here with some officers. They searched the whole place and talked to all of us. They took Clive to the station house for an interview." It was only on that last sentence that her voice broke and the strain she had to be under, the suspicions she must have had, showed through.

"Are you going to the police station?" I wouldn't have been surprised if she'd been headed there, an expensive lawyer in tow.

"No." The steel was back in her voice. "I'm going to the hospital to see my mother."

As I removed my coat and boots, a mournful piano tune came from the living room. I opened the double doors. "Jake, we need to talk."

He stopped playing immediately and closed the cover over the keyboard. He kept his head bowed over the piano and didn't turn to look at me.

"I know it was you who sent the Black Widow to my mother."

His head hung farther, but he didn't deny it. "How did you know?"

I moved Marguerite's straight-backed chair and placed it across from the piano bench. I sat down, leaning forward. Jake turned so he and I were face to face. "Hugh told Tallulah he'd 'taken care of it,'" I said. "He would have asked someone he trusted to mail the necklace. Paolo says it wasn't him, and I believe him. Rose didn't get to Boston until after it was mailed. Tallulah doesn't know what happened to it, and Marguerite didn't know it was in the house. Hugh wouldn't have trusted Vivian or Clive. Paolo has told me how close you were. Hugh trusted you."

We sat quietly for a moment. "Why didn't you tell Tallulah?" I asked.

Jake's voice was barely above a whisper. "Hugh asked me not to."

"But why did he send it without any explanation? Why all the secrecy, with no return address and the zip code obscured?" In spite of my best intentions, my voice rose, accusing.

mother. It's on the desk in our room under a bunch of papers. Please get it. It's time to give it to her."

Rose looked at me. "You've got to get going to the airport. If you and your boyfriend don't make it out before this next snow, it could be days."

I caught up with her in the hallway. "How did you know what he was going to say?" I asked.

She shook her wavy hair. "Are you kidding? I could tell by the look on his face. And on yours. But how did you know? How did you figure it out?"

"Detective Salinsky kept asking who benefited from the timing of Hugh's death. I realized only one person did. Hugh. His pain finally ended."

Hugh had done everything he needed to do, including reaching out to my mother. Paolo just didn't know it.

Chapter 34

The sky was gray by the time I pulled the pickup in front of the terminal at Logan airport. Chris was at the curb, shivering in a lightweight jacket. Despite my irritation about the "no reason to be in Maine," remark, my heart beat faster when I saw his long legs, tousled brown hair, and green eyes. It had been one helluva week. I needed his strong arms around me.

He slid his carry-on bag behind the passenger seat and climbed in. We kissed while the airport cop glared and waved, indicating we'd taken too much time at the curb.

"How was your trip?" I asked.

"Middle seat from Charlotte, but I was lucky to get out. Rough roads ahead. Sure you're okay to drive?"

"Positive. For now."

"Good." He lay his head against the window. Before we were out of the city, he was asleep.

The days and nights in Key West must have been even wilder than I'd imagined.

The snow started up again by the time we hit Route 95. There weren't many cars on the road. The envelope Tallulah had given me before I left sat in my tote bag. The outside said simply, "Jacqueline," in the shaky handwriting of the infirm. The bold lettering on the substituted note, "For Windsholme," had been written by Jake. The envelope was sealed, and though I burned to know what was in it, Hugh's trust had been violated once already when Jake waylaid the letter. I wasn't going to do it again.

Just south of the New Hampshire border, the snow was really coming down. My phone rang. Chris startled from sleep. "What, what?"

"It's Mom." I handed him the phone. "Put her on speaker so I can drive with two hands."

"Julia?" The slight tremor in Mom's voice sent a shiver up my spine.

"What's wrong?"

"This is really it. Sonny was in Wiscasset at the supermarket shopping for his dad. He turned around right away when I reached him, but I'm afraid it'll be slow going because of the storm. As soon as he gets here, he'll take your sister to the hospital. Page and I will stay here. We can't all fit in the truck and there's no sense in having two vehicles out in this weather."

"How close is Livvie? Should you call an ambulance?"

"With this snow, I'd rather she was in Sonny's truck than the ambulance."

"But the ambulance comes with trained—"
The elegant efficiency of the EMTs who'd come
to the house on Marlborough Street the night
before was engraved in my memory.

"Livvie says she can wait."

"Okay. Keep me posted."

"You too. Check in again from the road,
please."

"Will do."

We said our good-byes and Chris clicked off
my phone. He stared forward at the windshield,
where white flakes careened out of a white sky,
to be whisked away by the wipers. "You okay to
keep driving? I'm feeling pretty good after
that nap."

"I don't want to stop yet. I'll let you know."

He shifted in his seat. "When it gets dark, the
road will freeze."

I nodded to show I understood and leaned
farther forward toward the steering wheel, like
those few inches would help me navigate. We'd
crossed into New Hampshire while I'd talked to
Mom and now were nearly to Portsmouth.

"Can I ask you something?" Chris said.

Despite the road conditions, I stole a glance
at his strong profile. His eyes were on the road.
"Sure."

"Are you upset with me?"

So there it was. The thing there'd been no
time to discuss or dissect. The thing I wasn't
sure I even wanted to examine. My first instinct
was to dodge. "It's been an exhausting three
days. I met a whole family I didn't know I had,

found out my mother's cousin Hugh was alive, but then dead, saw an elderly cousin carried out of her house to an ambulance, and maybe even survived an attack on my life."

"What!" Chris stomped his foot on the floor of the truck, as if to slam the brakes on the conversation.

"I told you about my panic attack on Tuesday night, right?" I couldn't remember what I had and hadn't told him.

"No." A look of pained concern. "It's been a long time since you've had one."

"Months. And this one didn't feel 'normal.'" *Like panic attacks are ever normal.* "The theory is that Marguerite was given an overdose of her own beta-blocker. I think maybe someone slipped me some as well, either on purpose, or more likely accidentally, trying to poison Marguerite. I took the wrong glass."

"Julia, what are you talking about?"

It took a while to fill him in. On the white road, tracks of bare pavement created by earlier vehicles disappeared under our wheels as we rode along. After I'd finished talking, when Chris didn't say anything, I looked over. He was frozen in place, turned toward me. Only his eyes were alive with love and concern. "Julia."

"It's okay. I'm okay."

"It's not okay. I love you. I can't imagine my life without you."

"I'm right here."

We'd crossed the Piscataqua River Bridge into Maine, buffeted by gusts of wind. Along the highway, warning signs flashed, reducing the speed limit to thirty. My shoulders hurt from the tension and the concentration required to drive in the storm.

"At least it's nothing I did," Chris said. "I thought you were upset with me." He was relaxed enough to smile.

"I *was* upset with you. Kind of. A little." I tried to keep my voice light. He'd just told me he loved me, for goodness' sake.

"Out with it. What did I do?"

"When you called from Key West, you said you were thinking of living outside Busman's Harbor for the first time ever."

"So?"

"So? I turned my life inside out and upside down to stay in Busman's Harbor to be with you, and now you're thinking of moving somewhere else?"

Chris's deep chuckle was easy, untroubled. "Staying is a fantasy nearly everyone has in the Keys. Emphasis on the word 'fantasy.'" He reached across the cab and put his hand on my thigh. "If you don't know by now that I want to spend the rest of my life with you, I don't know when you're going to get it."

"Well," I said, "you've never said that before."

"I didn't think I needed to."

Chapter 35

When we stopped at the Kennebunk rest area for coffee and to switch drivers, I called my mother.

"Sonny's here," she said. "He put the truck in a ditch and had to walk the last two miles. We're waiting for the ambulance." In the background, I heard my sister moan. "I don't think you and Chris should come. Driving is too dangerous. Stay where you are."

"We're coming."

She sighed. "All right. Call me when you get closer and I'll tell you whether to come here or go to the hospital."

"Will do."

On our way out the door of the rest stop, a state trooper told us the highway was closed north of Bangor.

"Not going that far," Chris told him. "But thanks."

The trooper nodded, knocking off the snow

that had accumulated on the brim of his hat during his short walk across the nearly empty parking lot. "Good luck. Go slow."

We crept out onto the deserted highway, the snow showering down in the high streetlights. Chris drove steadily and cautiously. The plows and the sanders were keeping up, but as we passed the first Brunswick exit, a car fifty feet ahead caught a tire in the deeper snow between the lanes and fishtailed wildly. Chris braked the truck carefully as the car went into a full spin and ended up by the side of the road, facing the way it had been traveling.

Chris stopped beside the car and I opened my window. "You okay?"

"Ayuh," the man answered, though his lips were the same color as his pale, pale skin. "Just shaken up. I'll sit here a spell."

I saw the lights of a Maine state cruiser in our rearview mirror. "Good luck getting home, man," Chris shouted, and accelerated away.

When we pulled off our exit, the truck strained for traction in the deeper snow, struggling to get us up the ramp. I called Mom again to tell her we were off the highway. No answer. Fear grabbed my stomach and rolled it into a ball. If she was at the house with Page, and Livvie and Sonny were safely at the hospital, Mom would have pounced on her phone.

Chris cautioned me against jumping to conclusions. "Cell tower could be down."

I wasn't sure what conclusion to jump to. Was

Mom too busy to answer the phone because she was delivering Livvie's baby?

"I can't go any faster," he added.

"I know." We were on Route 1, which was not nearly as well plowed as the highway, and the closer we got to the ocean, the more the wind screamed. There were times when I couldn't see three feet in front of us. Blurry lights shown from houses off the side of the road. I wondered if we should stop. If a car, or worse, a truck, was stopped, stuck in the road ahead, I doubted Chris would see it in time to brake. I closed my eyes, taking big breaths to slow my racing pulse.

The trip over the top of the high Sagadahoc Bridge from Bath to Woolwich was terrifying. The wind bounced the heavy truck around like a tin can, and we slid a little going down the other side. Chris cursed and slowed even more.

When we turned off Route 1 to go down our peninsula, there were no lights anywhere. Not in the houses, or the road, not in the filling stations, which were locked up tight. Halfway down the peninsula, Chris stopped at an empty intersection. It was completely dark. There was about six inches of snow in the main road, but almost a foot on the side road. "You have to decide now. Hospital or Livvie's house?"

I'd thought about little else since we'd turned off Route 1. If any road in town had been kept clear, it would be the access road to the hospital. But, if Livvie was there, she didn't need our help. "To their house."

Chris took a left. The truck screamed in protest

as he pushed it onward. We were almost past Sonny's truck when I spotted it, angled into a snowbank. And then, half a mile beyond that, an empty ambulance and cop car stopped in the road, lights still flashing. "Oh, my God."

"We have to get out." Chris's voice was steady and firm. "We can make it from here."

I slid out of the passenger side door, making a soft landing on the snow-covered road. I was dressed in jeans, warm socks, and Bean boots. I had my down coat, with my hat and gloves in the pockets, but I wasn't really prepared for this kind of weather, Chris even less so. He fished his winter coat out from behind the seat and put it on. I was grateful to see he had gloves and a ski hat in his pockets.

Livvie and Sonny lived in a cul-de-sac, a neighborhood of split level houses owned in equal parts by young families and retirees, almost all of them year-round. "Follow that." Chris pointed to a rapidly filling trench in the snow, no doubt where the police officer from the cruiser and the EMTs had run, carrying their equipment.

It was hard walking, progress slow, but when I finally spotted the dark silhouette of the house, I broke into a run, imagining the worst. The front door was unlocked.

"Julia!"

"Page!" She flung herself into my arms. I couldn't tell if she was shivering because she was scared or because my wet coat was making her cold, but I let her cling for a moment. "Where's your mom?"

And then I heard it from upstairs, the high-pitched wail of a newborn. I took the stairs two at a time. Livvie was in her bed, hair slicked to her head with sweat, bathed in the emergency lights the EMTs must have carried from the ambulance. My mother was on the other side of the bed wiping her eyes. Sonny was behind her, a goofy grin on this face. Two EMTs, a man and a woman, packed up equipment. Our friend Jamie stood in his uniform, looking shell-shocked, like someone had sucker-punched him between the eyes.

Livvie gestured with her chin to the bundle in her arms. "Julia. Come meet your nephew, John. John Morrow Ramsey. John for Dad. Morrow for Mom's family."

And so we went on.

Chapter 36

Mom squinted at the vanilla-colored stationery in the faint light coming in through Livvie's front picture window. Livvie, the baby, John, and Sonny had gone to the hospital at last in an ambulance escorted by a convoy of plows. Chris and Page were asleep upstairs. The power was still off.

As she read, Mom pinched the bridge of her nose to hold back the tears, until she gave up and let them flow freely. I retrieved a box of tissues from the powder room. She took it and wordlessly handed me the letter.

My Dearest Jacqueline—

I can imagine your surprise and your anger when you receive this letter. Know this—I never meant to hurt you. Or perhaps I did, the first day of my disappearance, or the second, but no more than that. It is true I did not wish to see

*you, at least the first few years, but that was for
my own protection.*

*When we fought that night of your birthday,
when I told you your determination to marry
John Snowden would bring you nothing but
misery, I meant every word I said. I am so
sorry the last words I ever spoke to you were in
anger and bitterness. And I am so glad, now,
you ignored me.*

*I said some terrible things about John that
night, about his lack of prospects, lack of
education, his utter inability to give you the
life of comfort I thought you deserved, the life
of the mind I knew you needed. I'd convinced
myself I believed what I said about John, those
horrible, snobbish sentiments. But they were a
cover, designed to advance my own agenda.*

*I was in love with you. You are the only
woman I ever loved.*

Perhaps you knew?

*Perhaps you didn't. You saw me then as
you always did, as the brother you'd never
had, the best pal, the faithful friend. I was
all those things to you. I will be forever grateful
for everything you and Uncle Gerald gave me,
because it was so much. Most of all, more than
anything, you gave me a home, a safe and
welcoming place so unlike my parents' house.
Others may have found Uncle Gerald remote,
but as his daughter, you know better. You know
he taught me to fish, to sail, to bird watch,
everything that later became important in my*

*life. He gave me the time and attention my
father never did.*

*And you. You were the adoring sister,
and the partner in crime, the person who
held all my secrets. Except the one. Except the
knowledge that I adored you and thought every
moment about spending my life with you. We
are third cousins after all, barely related.*

*I told myself for the longest time John was a
passing fancy. He was so different from you in
every way. I understood the attraction, but was
sure it would fade. It wasn't until the night of
your twenty-first birthday that I understood
you were serious and meant to make a life with
him. I was so angry. I lashed out and said
terrible things. Things that cause me pain and
embarrassment even today. Even as I lie dying.*

*That is why I snuck away on the boat that
night. That is why I never let you know I was
alive. At first I was angry, and then I was
embarrassed, and then it was too late.*

*I have watched you over the years, as
an unseen but caring presence. I rejoiced
when your daughters were born and your
granddaughter. I have marveled at your
success, and John's, in building a business
that kept Morrow Island in your family and
provided a life for you all. I mourned when
your father died, for your loss and my own,
and again when John was taken much too
young.*

*You will wonder about the contents of
this package. I haven't seen you in more*

*than three decades, but I believe I still know
you well enough to predict your reaction.
You will question whether you deserve the
Black Widow, if you should accept it. I'm not
sure what will persuade you, so let me try this:
the necklace was my parents', and before that
my grandparents'. But before that, it belonged
to our mutual great-great-great-grandparent,
so it is as much yours as mine. I have no
earthly need of it, and soon no heavenly need
of it, either.*

*When you get this, you will not only be
furious at my deception, you will be angry
I kept the family from you, not just later, but
even during our years together. Why did I
never mention Rose and her mother, or
Marguerite and Vivian, whom I was just
coming to know back then? The answer is, I
don't know. Sometimes I think I was preparing
even then for a life of compartmentalization
and separation, a thousand little rehearsals
for the life I ultimately led. I am sorry for it
now. Of all the many things, it is the one for
which I am the sorriest.*

*It is my hope that you will sell the Black
Widow. She has been hidden from anyone's
enjoyment for generations. I have otherwise
provided for our cousin Marguerite Morales,
who will provide for her daughter, Vivian,
and granddaughter, Tallulah. My brother
Arthur's daughter, Rose, also understands my
intentions. I want you to rebuild Windsholme.
I have read of the tragic fire there and seen the*

photos. You and your children are the guardians of it now, and it should stand, strong and straight, against the North Atlantic.

As you rebuild Windsholme, it is also my hope you will rebuild the family. It was the Black Widow that tore us apart originally, and I believe putting it to rights will bring us together. Let this letter be an introduction for you to the rest of your family.

By the time you receive this package, I will be gone. Despite your anger and shock, you may regret you did not get to see me one last time, but I have not risen from the dead for you to see me as I am. I want you always to remember me sailing away from the dock on Morrow Island, a young man, handsome and strong, laughing and buoyed by your love, even when it was not the kind of love I wished for. Though you would not know it to see me today, I am that man still.

      With Love,
      Hugh

Chapter 37

It was April before we could find a time to be together to place the urn containing Hugh's ashes in the family vault. The day was unseasonably warm and the paths at Mount Auburn Cemetery wound through the pale greens of early spring, accompanied by the occasional slash of yellow from a forsythia bush.

Marguerite sat in a wheelchair, pushed by Vivian. I could imagine the scene when Vivian insisted her mother ride, not walk, to Hugh's burial.

Clive wasn't there and no one spoke of him. Detective Salinsky continued to build a case against him for the attempted murder of Marguerite, while others across law enforcement looked into his past deeds. The problem wasn't a lack of charges, but too many. Clive was even younger than I'd thought, barely twenty-seven. For a relatively young man, he'd left a trail of broken promises, hearts, and fortunes. I asked

Salinsky why twelve women had married him, and why so many people, old, young, male, and female, had given him money for his nonexistent companies.

"They did it because he was bold enough to ask," Salinsky said. "Happens all the time."

When the possible charges had come to light, Clive had slunk out of the house on Marlborough Street with only the suitcase he'd brought with him. At least Marguerite hadn't had to pay him to go away. Perhaps there was some solace in that.

Tallulah wore a sleeveless black dress with her tattoos showing in all their glory. It was a warm day for April, but April in New England nonetheless. Perhaps she had some source of body heat none of the rest of us possessed. Her eyes were ringed in their usual black.

Jake fussed around her, the caring husband I knew him to be. Mr. Dickison had found him a crackerjack criminal lawyer. Jake had turned himself in, but was out on bail while the attorneys negotiated a plea deal. Euthanasia was illegal in Massachusetts, but there were no witnesses and the family of the victim was solidly behind him. I was the only person Jake had confessed to, presumably aside from his lawyer. He had never said the words to me, exactly, and though I'd understood his meaning, I was grateful, in case I ever had to testify.

Rose brought her husband, a tall, handsome,

African-American doctor, and their son. He was not quite as tall as his father, and gangly, an L-shaped teenager not yet grown into his feet. When my mother met him at the chapel, she held both his hands in her own. "You look just like him," she said, her eyes filling. "Just like your Uncle Hugh." It had taken me a moment to see it. Photos didn't capture Hugh's expressions or gestures, but Marguerite backed Mom up.

"He does!" she agreed. "I'd never noticed before. You'll be a handsome man," she assured the blushing teen.

Livvie, Sonny, and Page were there, with John Morrow Ramsey in a sling across Livvie's belly. He was a mellow baby, cheerfully cooperative about long car rides and unfamiliar faces cooing over him. He'd been born bald as a cue ball, and still was, no sign of Sonny's fiery temper or red hair.

Chris had come too, and I was happy to have his reassuring presence behind me as we approached the family vault. In the past few months we'd both grown more comfortable talking about the future, "this summer," "next Christmas," "next year." We had turned another corner, and happily so.

The family plot featured an elaborate Victorian monument, which entombed Lemuel and first wife, Sarah. The vault containing the ashes of other family members stood beside it. Marguerite's mother was there, along with distant ancestors too numerous to count. Many were missing too; generations of Rose's family were buried in San Francisco, along with her father, mother, and grandparents. My grandmother was buried in Busman's Harbor, along with my grandfather Gerald, a man I appreciated more for having seen him through Hugh's final letter.

"This is a crazy family," Page had complained in the car on the ride to the cemetery, after I'd attempted to clarify who was who. But as I looked at us, infant and ancient, single, married, divorced, and widowed, brown skinned, olive skinned, freckled and pale, I thought, *most American families are like this.*

We stood in a semicircle while a cemetery employee put Hugh's urn in the vault, and then Tallulah sang, "*All I ask, all I want is this, if you loved me, love one another when I'm gone.*"

Her voice was mournful, husky, and fully in her command. As she took her trained singer's breaths, the little gray bird tattooed on her chest came alive, and it too appeared to sing, full throated and wholehearted. I looked at Livvie standing across from me. Neither of us had ever met Hugh, but our eyes ran with tears.

We had lunch at the Harvard Club. There was much catching up to do and never a lag in the conversation, and then Mom, Vivian, Rose, and I left for Skinner's for the auction of the Black Widow.

Hugh had intended to leave it to my mother alone, but there was no doubt Vivian would challenge her ownership, and Cuthie Cuthbertson had urged us to reach an agreement rather than face litigation. At my mother's insistence, Rose was included too. The money from the necklace would be split evenly by the three families. Rose pointed out that her branch had benefited from the capital it had secured for five generations, but Mom was undeterred.

The Black Widow was the main attraction of the day, though the bidding was brisk on the magnificent antique jewelry pieces that led up to its sale. When the necklace came up for auction, a dapper gentleman in a black suit and black mustache led off the bidding. He was quickly bid up by a woman in an elegant red dress and another person on the phone. The auction employee who had handled our sale told us keen interest from multiple parties would be the key to maximizing the Black Widow's potential value.

Rose, Mom, Vivian, and I held hands, and our collective breath, as the bids flew by us: 2 million, 2.1, 2.2. The woman in the red dress dropped out, but the mustachioed man and mystery person on the phone kept bidding: 2.5 million . . . 3 million . . . 4.

The audience, which had been sedate all afternoon, buzzed with conversation. The auction house employees around the room stared at one another, their looks as puzzled as our own.

I squeezed Mom's hand on one side and Rose's on the other. If they hadn't been there to hold me up, I might have fallen over.

The auctioneer kept going: 4.5 million, 4.75. The bidding slowed, the increments became smaller. At last the man with the mustache signaled he was through.

The auctioneer brought down his gavel. Five million dollars to the person on the phone.

We hugged and cried and hugged some more. There would be the auction house, Massachusetts inheritance tax, and the lawyers to pay, but still, even split three ways, there would be enough money to restore Windsholme. Mr. Dickison had been clear that Hugh's final wishes for how my mother spent the money were in no way binding, but she was determined. She'd already contacted my friend Quentin, who'd long been a proponent of rebuilding the house, and he had found "the perfect architect, who would respect its neocolonial style while making it a modern place to live."

I was skeptical. The Snowden Family Clambake had barely escaped bankruptcy the year before. I wanted to pay off the money Quentin had loaned us, but he wouldn't hear of it, and I could see my mother was not to be deterred. It wasn't my money, or my house, so I kept my mouth shut. For now.

Back at the house on Marlborough Street, we had a dinner of Rose's lasagna. The wine flowed throughout our loud celebration. Everyone's life story spilled out in a series of questions and answers.

Marguerite sat at the head of the table, the dreaded wheelchair put away for the moment. Toward the end of the meal she cleared her throat and raised her glass. The conversation died and she spoke. "A toast to Hugh, the child of my heart, who brought us all together in the end."

We raised our glasses too. "Hear, hear," we chorused. "To Hugh."

Recipes

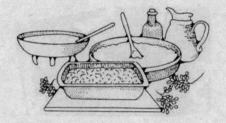

Vee's Beef Stew

One of my most precious possessions is a book of handwritten recipe cards given to me by my maternal grandmother, Ethel McKim. When I planned for Julia and her mother to be snowed in, I knew I would turn to this book full of comfort foods for many of the recipes. This one is made by Vee Snugg in the book, and it's as homey and delicious as you might imagine. I have provided amounts for the vegetables, though according to my grandmother's note, you can use as many or as few as you please.

INGREDIENTS

2 pounds of beef, cubed
6 carrots, cut in three inch chunks
4 medium potatoes, peeled and cut in half
1 15-ounce jar pearl onions, drained
1 3-ounce can tomato sauce
3 ounces of water
1 teaspoon sugar
Juice of ½ lemon
3 Tablespoons instant tapioca
Salt and pepper
6 drops Worcestershire sauce

INSTRUCTIONS

In a bowl, mix well tomato sauce, water, sugar, lemon juice, instant tapioca, and Worcestershire sauce.

In a casserole dish, pile meat in center. Place all vegetables around the edges. Pour tomato mixture over all. Cover and cook in a preheated oven at 225 degrees for 6 to 7 hours. Can be prepared in advance and reheated. Makes a delicious brown sauce.

Serves 4 to 6.

Ma's Ginger Snaps

When my cousins get together, one memory we all share is my grandmother's ginger snaps. It was a joy to find them in your mailbox at camp, or on a bluesy day in your college dorm. They always came in a coffee can, lined on the inside with wax paper and taped shut. The cookies provided instant comfort and could be hoarded or shared, depending on your mood.

INGREDIENTS

1½ sticks butter, melted
2 cups granulated white sugar
¼ cup molasses
1 egg, beaten lightly
2 cups flour
1 teaspoon baking soda
½ teaspoon ginger
¼ teaspoon each cloves, allspice, nutmeg,
    mace
1 teaspoon cinnamon
½ teaspoon salt

INSTRUCTIONS

Mix the melted butter, 1 cup of the sugar, and the molasses. (Put aside the remaining cup of sugar.) When the mixture is cool, fold in the lightly beaten egg. In another bowl, mix the flour, baking soda, ginger, cinnamon, salt, cloves, allspice, nutmeg, and mace. Add the dry ingredients to the wet. Mix thoroughly with a mixer or food processor.

Dough will form itself into a ball. Wrap in plastic wrap and put into refrigerator for at least 4 hours or overnight.

Shape cold dough into balls using a small melon baller. Roll the balls in sugar to coat completely. Place the balls at least 2 inches apart on parchment paper on a cookie sheet, to allow for expansion.

Bake in a preheated oven at 350 degrees for 10 to 12 minutes.

Jacqueline's Meat Loaf

Jacqueline Snowden isn't much of a cook, but she can manage this simple meat loaf. This is one that I made for my kids a lot when they were growing up.

INGREDIENTS

2 pounds ground beef
1 medium onion, diced
1½ cups dried Italian bread crumbs
1 egg
½ cup ketchup
2 Tablespoons Dijon mustard

INSTRUCTIONS

Combine all ingredients in a bowl and work with your hands until thoroughly mixed. (It's a cold, messy job, but somebody's got to do it!) Form the mixture into a loaf. Cook in an oven preheated to 375 degrees for 45 minutes.

Serves 6.

Rose's Three-Cheese Lasagna

Rose's lasagna is the one a college roommate taught me to make. All these years later, it remains one of my specialties. Somehow I have even become the lasagna maker for our Easter celebrations with my husband's large Italian-American family. Though in fairness, I have to acknowledge that my husband makes the sauce.

INGREDIENTS FOR THE SAUCE

4 28-ounce cans Italian tomatoes
    (preferably San Marzano)
4 6-ounce cans tomato paste
2 Tablespoons olive oil, divided
5 pounds sweet Italian sausage (20 to
    24 links, depending on size)
6 ounces pancetta, diced
2 medium onions, chopped
2 red bell peppers, diced
4 medium cloves garlic, chopped
1 cup red wine
1 teaspoon dried oregano
1 teaspoon dried basil
salt and pepper

INSTRUCTIONS FOR THE SAUCE

Crush the tomatoes or quickly puree in a blender.

Heat a large saucepan over medium high heat and add 1 Tablespoon of the olive oil. Prick the sausages in several places with a fork. Working in batches so the sausages brown and don't steam, brown the sausages on all sides. Set browned sausages aside in a bowl.

Drain the pan of fat, return to the heat, and add the second Tablespoon of olive oil and the pancetta. Cook the pancetta until nearly crispy and add the onions and peppers. Sauté for 7 minutes. Add the garlic. Cook another 1 to 2 minutes, until the garlic becomes fragrant. Add the wine and stir constantly to deglaze the pan. Let the wine cook down for 2 to 3 minutes, then add the tomato paste and stir constantly for about 2 minutes to distribute throughout the vegetables. Add the canned tomatoes and stir. Return the sausages and any accumulated juices to the sauce. Add the oregano, basil, and salt and pepper. Bring the sauce up to a simmer. Partially cover the pan and simmer for 2 hours. Adjust seasonings, if needed.

Make the sauce a day ahead if possible.

INGREDIENTS FOR LASAGNA

27 no boil lasagna noodles
3 24-ounce containers whole milk ricotta
3 pounds mozzarella cheese
2 cups grated Romano cheese, divided
2 eggs
3 pounds ground beef
1 medium onion, diced
1 bunch of Italian parsley

Instructions for the Lasagna

In a large frying pan, combine the ground beef and the diced onion. Cook until the meat is lightly browned.

In a food processor, combine ricotta cheese, 1 cup of the Romano cheese, the eggs, and the tops from the entire bunch of Italian parsley. I create this mixture in two batches due to the quantity.

Remove the sweet Italian sausages from the sauce and slice them. I use the slicing attachment on my food processor. It's a messy, imprecise process, but no one will know!

Shred the mozzarella cheese. I use the grater attachment on my food processor.

In a large (16 x 13 x 4) roasting pan, layer

    Sauce to lightly cover the bottom of the
       pan
    ⅓ of the noodles
    ½ of the ricotta mixture
    ½ of the ground beef. Use a slotted spoon
       to leave most fat in the pan.
    ½ of the sliced sausage
    ½ of the mozzarella
    Sauce to lightly cover the layer
    ⅓ of the noodles
    ½ of the ricotta mixture

½ of the ground beef. Use a slotted spoon
   to leave most fat in the pan.
½ of the sliced sausage
½ of the mozzarella
⅓ of the noodles
Sauce to lightly cover the noodles
Romano cheese sprinkled across the top

Cover the pan with aluminum foil, shiny side
down. Preheat the oven to 350 degrees and
bake for 2 hours.

Serve with the remaining sauce, heated, and the
Romano cheese on the side.

Serves many

The Daily Catch Lobster Fra Diavolo

I include a lobster recipe in every Maine Clambake Mystery, and since this book takes place in the off-off-season, I knew Julia would eat the lobster meal at a restaurant on her visit to Boston. From there, it was an easy decision to have that meal take place at the Daily Catch, my favorite seafood restaurant. Second-generation Chef Basil Freddura (completely coincidentally an old camp buddy of my daughter's) kindly offered up three signature recipes. The Daily Catch has three locations. The one where Marguerite, Rose, and Julia go is in the Seaport district, though I served them a dessert only on the menu in the Brookline location.

INGREDIENTS FOR DAILY CATCH SEAFOOD MARINARA SAUCE

1 #10 can (6 pounds, 9 ounces) crushed
   tomatoes
4 Tablespoons olive oil
4 bulbs garlic, peeled and rough chopped
1 white onion, peeled and rough
   chopped
1 carrot, peeled and rough chopped
½ Tablespoon dried oregano
½ Tablespoon dried basil
½ Tablespoon fennel seed
1 teaspoon salt
1 teaspoon pepper
1 pound lobster bodies
1 cup water

INSTRUCTIONS FOR SEAFOOD MARINARA SAUCE
(MAKE A DAY AHEAD.)

In a large pot cook over medium-high heat the olive oil, garlic, onion, carrot, spices, lobster bodies, and water. Let simmer for about 30 minutes until flavors have had a chance to come together.

Add to the pot the crushed tomatoes and rinse out the can with a bit more water and add that too. Continue to cook the sauce over medium-high heat, stirring frequently. Once sauce reaches a simmer, reduce heat to low and simmer for 2 to 3 hours, stirring occasionally throughout that time.

Once finished cooking, remove sauce from heat and allow to cool to room temp for another hour or so, stirring occasionally. Transfer the sauce into a container large enough and store in the fridge overnight.

The next day, the sauce is ready to strain. Pour sauce into a colander with a bowl or pot underneath to catch the strained sauce. With a large spoon or whisk, stir the sauce around the colander, forcing it to strain through and into the new pot or container. Once most of the liquid has gone through the colander and all you have are solids in strainer, add a touch of water and mix one last time to get every bit of flavor out of the bodies. By now, all you should have is lobster bodies and tomato pulp in the strainer; these can be discarded as their job is done! This sauce is now ready for the Lobster Fra Diavolo!

Note: You will use 4 cups of the sauce for Lobster Fra Diavolo (below). You can freeze any remainder. It is excellent over pasta.

INGREDIENTS FOR
DAILY CATCH LOBSTER FRA DIAVOLO

2 1¼ pound live lobsters, body and tail
  cut in half, claws removed, and
  stomach discarded
12 littleneck clams, washed
1½ pounds PEI mussels, washed and
  beards removed
1 pound calamari, cut into rings and
  tentacles
12 shrimp, peeled and deveined
1 Tablespoon olive oil
½ Tablespoon crushed red pepper, add
  half or quarter amount if less spice
  desired
1 Tablespoon garlic, peeled and minced
¼ cup white wine
4 cups Seafood Marinara Sauce,
  see previous.
1 pound linguine pasta
1 Tablespoon Italian parsley

Instructions for Lobster Fra Diavolo

Bring a large pot of salted water to a rolling boil.

Heat olive oil, garlic, and crushed pepper over high heat in a large skillet or pot. Skillet should be at least 14 inches wide and 6 inches deep. If large skillet is unavailable, use large pot with well-fitting lid.

When garlic gets fragrant, 2 to 3 minutes, add littleneck clams and lobster pieces. Do not burn garlic. Deglaze with white wine. Add marinara sauce and cover. Simmer for 3 to 5 minutes or until sauce begins to boil, stirring often.

Once sauce boils, add mussels, shrimp, and calamari and stir until all the seafood is evenly distributed in the pot. Replace cover and continue to cook.

Drop the linguine into boiling water and cook until desired doneness, 4 to 6 minutes, stirring often.

Once all the clams and mussels pop open, and all the seafood is cooked, turn off heat and wait for linguine to finish cooking.

When linguine is done, place in large serving bowl or pan. Ladle some sauce and mix into pasta. Place all seafood on top of pasta in an organized fashion. Pour remaining sauce over pasta. Sprinkle parsley over top.

Serves 4.

Daily Catch Monkfish Marsala

*Once I knew I would set a scene in the story at the
Daily Catch, I couldn't resist including my favorite
dish there, Monkfish Marsala, which is also a signature dish.*

INGREDIENTS FOR
DAILY CATCH MONKFISH MARSALA

1 pound monkfish filets, trimmed and cut
   into thin medallions
½ Tablespoon olive oil
½ Tablespoon canola oil
1 cup flour
½ pound white mushrooms, sliced
1 cup Marsala wine
1 lemon, juiced
1 Tablespoon butter
salt and pepper
½ Tablespoon Italian parsley, chopped

INSTRUCTIONS FOR MONKFISH MARSALA

Heat the olive oil and canola oil over high heat
in a large pan, until just about smoking.

Season the monkfish medallions with salt and
pepper and dredge in the flour. Carefully place
the floured medallions in the hot pan and sear
until nice and golden brown.

Once browned, flip each piece and add the mushrooms. Cook for a minute until mushrooms begin to soften. Carefully deglaze the pan with the Marsala wine. The wine will ignite into a flame and continue to burn until all the alcohol has been cooked off. Gently shake the pan during this process to keep the flame going.

Once flame has finished, add lemon juice, salt, and pepper. Reduce heat to medium and continue to simmer and let Marsala wine reduce and monkfish cook. Once wine has thickened into a sauce, add the butter and gently swirl the pan as it melts. If sauce is too thick and not enough liquid is in pan, add a few drops of water. Once butter has melted and incorporated into sauce, remove from heat and serve. Garnish with chopped parsley.

Serves two

Acknowledgments

Pieces of Julia's mother's story have been told in each of the Maine Clambake Mysteries. We know Jacqueline lost her mother young, that she inherited Morrow Island, and that her once-wealthy ancestors build Windsholme. Her missing cousin, Hugh, is mentioned in the very first book in the series, *Clammed Up*. What we've never been told is how her family made their money and how they lost it. *Iced Under* supplies the missing pieces.

I've known for a while that the Morrows made their money in the frozen-water trade. The idea that New Englanders, in the early part of the nineteenth century, shipped ice halfway around the world has always seemed crazy to me. Crazy in an entrepreneurial, good way. Frederic Tudor was the originator of the ice trade, as well as the inventor of home iceboxes and frozen food. His extended family life was somehow even more colorful than his business. I borrowed a good deal of his history for Frederic Morrow. Two excellent books about Frederic Tudor are *The Ice King: Frederic Tudor and His*

Circle, by Carl Seaburg and Stanley Patterson (Massachusetts Historical Society and Mystic Seaport, 2003), and *The Frozen-Water Trade: A True Story*, by Gavin Weightman (Hyperion, 2003).

The end of the ice trade is as interesting as the beginning and brings us another fascinating character, Charlie Morse of Bath, Maine. I appropriated some of Charlie's deeds for William Morrow. If this novel has made you want to learn more, I recommend *Bath, Maine's Charlie Morse: Ice King & Wall Street Scoundrel*, by Philip H. Woods (The History Press, 2011).

I would like to thank my friend Mark Wilcox for suggesting the idea behind the GimmeThat! App, a Bitcoin for Uber for Millennials, and for taking the time to describe it to me. He's a million times smarter about technology than I am. I've dumbed the idea down, not for my readers' comfort, but for my own.

Carolyn Vandam walked me through the ins and outs of death and burial in Back Bay. I had to make some changes because, when the day came, I didn't have a body, but I was grateful to have a baseline.

A huge thank you to Basil Freddura, the chef at the Daily Catch in Boston's Seaport district, who supplied the recipes for Lobster Fra Diavolo and Monkfish Marsala, not to mention many wonderful evenings.

Julie Hennrikus, Ramona DeFelice Long, and Katrina Niidas Holm supplied critical information at just the right moments to keep me from making a fool of myself. If I have still managed to do so, it is no fault of theirs. I thank them all.

As always, I would like to thank my agent, John Talbot, as well as John Scognamiglio, Karen Auerbach, Robin Cook, and the whole team at Kensington, who have supported the entire Maine Clambake series.

Huge shout-outs to my writers group, Mark Ammons, Katherine Fast, Cheryl Marceau, and Leslie Wheeler, who reviewed a draft of the book and supplied valuable feedback. Thanks also to Sherry Harris, who supplied edits for this book while up against a deadline for her own series with Kensington, the Sarah Winston Garage Sale Mysteries.

My Wicked Cozy Authors blogmates are my lifeline every single day in this crazy writing life we share. Thank you, Jessica Estevao, Sherry Harris, Julianne Holmes, Maddie Day, and Liz Mugavero. And to my Mainers at the Maine Crime Writers Blog, especially Kaitlyn Dunnett, Lea Wait, and Kate Flora.

And finally, there is no possible way to thank my family enough for their support, but I will try. Bill Carito, Rob Carito, Sunny Carito, Viola Carito, Kate Donius, and Luke Donius, I couldn't do it without you. Love to you all.